UFOS AND LAW ENFORCEMENT

RESPONSE TO THE PHENOMENON

Book Domain LLC.
543 E Louise Dr Phoenix, Az 85050

Ordering Information:
Amount Deals. Special rebates are accessible on the amount bought by corporations, associations, and others. For points of interest, contact the distributor at the address above.

Printed in the United States of America.

ISBN-13   Paperback   978-1-967903-75-7
           eBook   978-1-967903-74-0

Library of Congress Control Number: 2025917589

UFOS AND LAW ENFORCEMENT

RESPONSE TO THE PHENOMENON

RAYMOND KELLER, PH.D.
FRED SALUGA

INTRODUCTION

By Christine M. Soltis.

When Fred Saluga contacted me about his upcoming book with Raymond Keller, I was delighted to hear that they were working on a book about aliens and law enforcement. When Fred Saluga asked me to write an introduction for the book using my own experiences in the topic matter, I was ecstatic and began to think of the details that very same day.

Since 2013, I have been involved in the investigative industry, specifically through private investigations in correlation to legal matters such as insurance red flags and potentially fraudulent activity. My full-time work has taken me throughout Pennsylvania, West Virginia, and Ohio on endless adventures, cases, and situations where one must act quickly in some cases or develop a plan of action that is basic survival for field investigations.

We are taught to de-escalate sometimes chaotic situations, which can be difficult to do during basic human interactions. This type of situation could possibly be quite terrifying if those chaotic encounters came to be with a non-human or extra-terrestrial entity instead. Fortunately, I have not personally encountered anything otherworldly during any of my field cases. We can't say the same for the poor souls you'll encounter in the pages ahead who may have ended up in situations with a species that they weren't quite expecting.

While my profession as a private investigator holds a very serious role, I am also well-involved in the paranormal and metaphysical communities. For decades, I have had a great interest in alien studies, the metaphysical, planetary information, and so much more! Through my companies, Solstice Night Sky Productions and Solstice Night Sky Designs, I carry out productions such as panel events, release books, and design jewelry and clothing with a paranormal and metaphysical edge.

You would be surprised to find how many current and former law enforcement individuals take an interest in studying what is both here and beyond our universe. We are an inquisitive species that likes to solve puzzles. When combining our research and investigative skills, we can study, and sometimes solve, the most inexplicable questions of the universe. From our universe to yours, please enjoy the pages ahead.

Sincerely,

Christine M. Soltis
Homestead, Pennsylvania
24 July 2025
SolsticeNightSky.com, Solstice Night Sky
Productions, Solstice Night Sky Designs

LAW ENFORCEMENT'S FIRST UFO ENCOUNTER

At the end of the 19th century, "airships" were the most commonly reported UFOs.

Within the borders of the United States, we must go back to the close of the 19th century to find a record of any law enforcement agent's first UFO encounter. For paranormal investigators, the years of 1891-1900 constituted the "Airship Era." There were literally thousands of reports of a mysterious airship crisscrossing the entirety of the continental United States during this period. But the only case on record involving law enforcement officers can be traced back to 6 May 1897 in the vicinity of the Blue Ouachita Mountain, immediately to the northwest of Hot Springs, Arkansas. Apart from this airship encounter, the only other claim to fame for this area is that President Bill Clinton's maternal grandfather was born here in 1898.

On the fateful day in question, Garland County Constable John J. Sumpter, Jr., and Deputy Sheriff John McLemore rode north out of Hot Springs on horseback, headed along a trail to Jessieville. This trail roughly corresponds to the contemporary Arkansas State Highway 7. They were headed to Jessieville to check out some alleged reports of cattle rustling. Along the way, the two lawmen witnessed a "brilliant light in the heavens." No sooner had they taken notice of the light, it blinked out. Since they were looking for suspected cattle rustlers, however, they didn't make any mention of the light, insofar as they didn't want to make any noise alerting any possible nearby thieves.

In Constable Sumpter's official report, he wrote that, "After riding four or five miles around through the hills, we again saw the light, which appeared to be much nearer to the earth. We stopped our horses and watched it coming down, until all at once it disappeared behind another hill. We rode on about half a mile further, when our horses refused to go further."

The strange light wasn't the only spooky aspect to this story. The Constable continued: "Almost a hundred yards distant, we saw two persons moving around with lights. Drawing our Winchesters- for we were now thoroughly aroused as to the importance or the situation- we demanded, 'Who is that, and what are you doing?'"

Then a middle-aged man with a long, dark beard stepped out from the trees. He held up a lantern in his right hand and asked the two riders to identify themselves. Once the bearded man was satisfied that Sumpter and McLemore were lawmen, he informed the Constable that, "I am here with two others, a young man and a woman. We have been traveling through the country in an airship."

In view of the airship, Constable Sumpter noted that, "We could plainly distinguish the outlines of the vessel, which was cigar-shaped and almost sixty-feet long, and looking just like the woodcut impressions that have been appearing in the newspapers recently." Even though it was dark and rainy, the Constable put in his report that he could see the young man about thirty yards away filling a big sack (a lister bag) with water, but that the woman was keeping back in the cover of darkness, holding an umbrella over her head.

The older, bearded gentleman, offered to take the two lawmen for a ride aboard the airship. "I can take you two anywhere you want to go, so long as it isn't raining." But the Constable replied, "That's OK, but we prefer to get wet."

In concluding his official report, the Constable wrote: "Asking the (bearded) man why the brilliant light was turned on and off so much, he replied that the light was so powerful that it consumed a great deal of his motive power. He said he would like to stop off in Hot Springs for a few days and take the hot baths, but his time was limited and he could not. He said they were going to wind up at Nashville, Tennessee, after thoroughly seeing the country.

"Being in a hurry, we left, and upon our return, about forty minutes later, nothing was to be seen. We did not hear or see the airship when it departed."

Source: ***Weekly World*** newspaper, Helena, Arkansas, 13 May 1897.

LAW ENFORCEMENT IN THE 1947 ROSWELL UFO CRASH COVER-UP

Chaves County, New Mexico, Sheriff George A. Wilcox and his two deputies played a significant role in facilitating the government's cover-up of the 1947 Roswell, New Mexico, UFO crash. Photo source: notizie.it

On the evening of 2 July 1947, several witnesses in and around Roswell, Chaves County, New Mexico, observed a shiny disc-shaped object wobbling and moving swiftly in a northwesterly direction through a dark cloudy sky. At daybreak on the following day, William Ware "Mack" Brazel, the foreman of the J. B. Foster Ranch located in Chaves County, on the outskirts of Roswell, 30 miles to the southeast of the small cattle town of Corona, situated in the adjacent Lincoln County, rode out on horseback to move sheep from one field to another. Accompanying him was a young neighbor boy, Timothy D. Proctor. As they rode, they came upon strange debris consisting of various-size chunks of a metallic material running from one hilltop, down an arroyo, up another hill, and running down the other side, all scattered across the range land property of the Foster Ranch. From the looks of the scene, it appeared as though some kind of aircraft had recently crashed there.

According to investigators from the Dr. J. Allen Hynek Center for UFO Studies (CUFOS) in Chicago, Illinois, Thomas J. Carey and Donald R. Schmitt, "Were it not for William Ware 'Mack' Brazel (1899-1963), there would never have been a Roswell Incident - at least not one known to the general public. In July 1947, the 48-year-old Brazel was scratching out a living as foreman of the J. B. Foster sheep ranch located 30 miles southeast of the small cattle town of Corona, New Mexico. The family lived in Tularosa, while Mack stayed on the ranch in a shack without a telephone, electricity, or even running water. The nearest neighbor was 10 miles."

Maggie and "Mack" Brazel from photograph taken in 1951, four years after Mack happened upon the debris of a crashed "aircraft" on range land in the outskirts of Roswell, New Mexico. Neighboring ranchers told Mack that he had a duty to inform the local Sheriff's Office about the crash site so they could dispatch a crew to determine what really happened out there and clean it up.

Brazel had heard something that sounded like an explosion the night before, but because it happened during a heavy rainstorm, he assumed that it must have been a loud thunderclap. But upon arriving at the debris site and picking up some of the metallic pieces, he realized that the loud noise was from the crash of this aircraft. He had never seen anything like this debris, all of it lightweight and durable with some pieces engraved with a type of "Egyptian hieroglyphics." Thinking that the metal might be from some experimental type of aircraft flying in or out of the Roswell Army Air Field, Brazel collected some of the strange metallic material and together with Timothy showed it to the young boy's parents, Floyd and Loretta Proctor, who advised their neighboring rancher Brazel to take the material into the Sheriff's Department in Roswell and present it to the Chaves County Sheriff George Wilcox, who would surely know what to do with it. When neighbor Floyd, a veteran of World War II, first got a glimpse of the material, he informed Mack Brazel that, "It looks way beyond my pay grade."

On 6 July 1947, Brazel loaded up some of the more interesting pieces of wreckage that he and Timothy came upon at the Foster Ranch into his pickup truck and drove them into Sheriff Wilcox' office in Roswell. Brazel was hoping that Wilcox might know what this material was and if he could find someone to help clear it all off the ranch property. Carey and Schmitt didn't think that the ranch foreman had any altruistic or patriotic motives in reporting the crash by turning in the material to the sheriff. In the two CUFOS investigators' estimation, Brazel only wanted Sheriff Wilcox to find out who was responsible for that "hot mess" out on the Foster Ranch and to follow up in getting somebody out there to clean it up.[1]

Anthony Bragalia, an independent UFO investigative journalist, opined on 6 September 2010 in the *UFOpro* yahoo group website[2] that, "Wilcox had no idea himself what the debris was that Mack had shown him. Skeptics gloss over a vital fact: Wilcox must have been sufficiently perplexed by the material- and sufficiently concerned about Mack's story- to then have immediately called military brass at the base requesting that they investigate. Wilcox must have firmly believed that something major had transpired. He had to have been told something or seen something so alarming that he chose to involve other authorities and contact busy Roswell Army Air Field (RAAF). And whatever it was that Mack showed George, it was

---

[1]   Thomas J. Carey and Donald R. Schmitt, "Mack Brazel Reconsidered," *International UFO Reporter* (Winter 1999), J. Allen Hynek Center for UFO Studies, Chicago, Illinois.

[2]   Received by Fred Saluga in e-mail from *UFOpro* yahoo group on 15 October 2010.

not a piece of a balloon or balloon train, as the government states. Wilcox had a first-hand familiarity with every manner of balloon. They fell with frequency on the ranchlands of the county that he served (Chaves). He would not have gotten hold of RAAF over something like balloon materials."

Photograph of Chaves County, New Mexico, Sheriff George A. Wilcox (1894-1961) making telephone call on 6 July 1947 to the military authorities at the Roswell Army Air Field (RAAF) to report a crashed "flying disk," as it appeared on the front page of the 9 July 1947 edition of the *Roswell Daily Record* newspaper, whose headline read, "Sheriff Wilcox Takes Leading Role in Excitement Over Report 'Saucer' Found."

Within five minutes of Wilcox making a call to the RAAF about this matter, military personnel descended upon the Chaves County Jail like white on rice. Army officers, in the same manner that they informed the Roswell City Fire Department employees that there was no need for them to go out to the crash site, also let Sheriff Wilcox and his deputies know that they, too, need not waste any time in going out to the site and assessing the situation. "It's best to leave these matters up to the aviation experts on the base," frankly emphasized a junior officer to the sheriff and his deputies.

SHERIFF WILCOX' INQUISITIVE DAUGHTERS

George and Inez Wilcox had two daughters, Phyllis and Elizabeth, both who were still alive in 2010, whom journalist Bragalia interviewed for his posting. By that time, the two daughters were married and retired professionals still living in New Mexico. Both very articulate, they declared that their father was "truly involved in an extraterrestrial event at Roswell in 1947," and Phyllis averred that, "Our dad (George Wilcox) felt cut out of the picture, and though it was his jurisdiction as the sheriff, he was compelled to cooperate. If he had to do it over, he would have told the press and reporters first, leaving the Army out of it."

**Phyllis McGuire, nee Wilcox (L), and younger sister Elizabeth
Tulk, nee Wilcox (R), as they appeared on the streets of Roswell,
New Mexico, in 2010. Photo: ufoexplorations.com**

From what Phyllis could recall of those Roswell days of yore, she said, "My father had some material with him, but I did not know what it was. He (her father) said that he had sent two deputies out there (to the crash site); and they had seen some things. They had seen a corral that had some of the material in it; and they had seen a large burnt spot on some grass about the size of a football field. The two deputies had found an area of blackened ground that appeared as if something large and circular had touched down.

"When I read in the Roswell paper about the flying saucer being found, I went into his (her father's) office to ask about it. I asked my father if he thought that the information about the saucer was true. He said, 'I don't know why Brazel would come all the way in here if there wasn't something to it.' He said Brazel brought in some of the material to show and that it looked like tinfoil, but when you wadded it up, it would come right back to its original shape. He felt it was an important finding and he sent deputies to investigate."

Here Phyllis confirmed the presence of the so-called "memory metal" that was brought into the County Jail by Brazel. She recalled that her father placed the strange metal in a wooden box within a small storage room in the jail. The sheriff's daughter was amazed at how some of the saucer debris exhibited the capacity of "remembering itself." This advanced characteristic was not incorporated by humans into any metals until decades later, when such an innovation proved useful to America's space program in the development of rockets and satellites.

Phyllis McGuire, in recollecting the momentous events that transpired at the jailhouse when Brazel brought in the saucer debris, said that she was told by the military personnel on the premises that she should leave the room while they discussed the matter with Brazel and her father. Later she would ask her father to fill her on some of the details of what really happened at that meeting, but Sheriff Wilcox refused to say anything about it. As Phyllis persisted with her questions, her mother Inez became flustered and blurted out, "Stop pestering your father. Just leave it alone!"

It wasn't until the early 1970s that Phyllis finally heard from her mother what occurred in the jailhouse on that most historic day. "What did Dad see that was so secret out there? Were there bodies, like so many of the townsfolk say?" the ever inquiring mind of daughter Phyllis wanted to know.

"There were alien bodies!" exclaimed mother Inez, adding that, "One was still alive when they were found, but it eventually died. They had large heads and eyes but small bodies. Dad felt sorry for them. I got the impression that they were not given good care, that they were treated as enemies."

Phyllis learned that her father had told her mother the whole story. "She (Inez) always knew. She didn't mention anyone else who was involved. They (the military personnel) said they would kill the whole family if anyone spoke the truth about it. And as for Dad, I think that he felt badly about not telling me anything about it. But then again, he might have been trying to protect us."

Wilcox' younger daughter Elizabeth Tulk also knew about the saucer crash and subsequent events surrounding it. She told Bragalia that, "In July 1947, I vited my parents in Roswell, New Mexico. On that day, when my husband Jay and I arrived, there were some jeeps and some Army Air Corps people at the County Jail. My husnamd asked my father what was going on and my father replied, 'Well, we had this man come in here saying there was this flying saucer and brought with him a piece of it. He said it looked like burned grass out where the material was found.'

"My mother would not talk about the event for years. However, as the years rolled along, my mother would say, 'Remember the time we had the flying saucer in Roswell?' I know of an article that Mom wrote and it said that we do not know to this day if it was a flying saucer because they told my father not to say a word."

Elizabeth recalls that the two deputies had already been dispatched to and gone out to the crash site before the military authorities had arrived at the jailhouse. When the deputies finally got back from the area designated by Brazel, they still had not located the specific crash site. What they did discover, however, was a "large circle-shaped blackened area that was baked hard." But when the deputies later tried to return to the area, the military had already cordoned it off and they were thus not able to see anything more. Husband Jay confirmed Elizabeth's account of the event.

The Wilcox daughters testimony of hearing about the "large blackened area" out at the crash site was also verified by RAAF officers Lewis Rickett and Chester Barton, who independently spoke of a "large burned or baked area." And the local Roswell undertaker, Glenn Dennis, mentioned seeing "metal pieces in the backs of trucks at the base that appered burned as if high heat were applied." This burning clue in the statements of others intimately associated with the event add credence to the accounts provided by the Wilcox daughters. The United States government has always maintained that what crashed at Roswell was just a military balloon, but balloons don't burn and bake gigantic circles in the middle of the desert.

SHERIFF WILCOX' GRANDDAUGHTER ATTESTS: "THEY WERE SPACE BEINGS!"

Even Sheriff Wilcox' granddaughter, the daughter of Elizabeth Tulk, Barbara Wilcox Dugger, was in on some of the bigger secrets pertaining to the Roswell UFO crash of 1947. After Sheriff Wilcox passed away in 1961, Barbara came to live with her widowed grandmother Inez, to assist her with household chores. Barbara quickly gained Inez' trust, who opened up to her more than she ever had to her mother Elizabeth. The granddaughter and others in the Wilcox family came to refer to Inez simply as "Big Mom." One day, while watching a television program where the subject of UFOs was mentioned, Barbara related that Big Mom started to "spill the beans" about the Roswell incident.

It all began with Big Mom turning to Barbara and inquiring, "Do you believe that there is life in outer space?"

Barbara replied, "Big Mom, you know that I do."

Then her grandmother continued, "Barbara, I must tell you something. But you must promise me that you will never talk about it to anyone else. Please keep this to yourself. When it all happened, the military police came to us in the Sheriff's Office and declared that if we, George and I, ever said a single word about the affair to anyone at all, they would kill not only us, but also the whole family."

"Big Mom, do you really believe that they (the military) would carry out such threats?" Barbara wanted to know.

Grandmother Inez somberly replied, "What do you think?"

Barbara Wilcox Dugger then continued with her statement about her grandmother, Big Mom: "She (Inez) said someone came to Roswell and told Mack (the sheriff) about the incident. My grandfather then went out to the site. It was in the evening and there was a big burned area, and he saw debris. He also saw four Space Beings. One of the little men was alive. Their heads were large. They wore suits like silk. After he (Mack) returned to his office, my grandfather got phone calls from all over the world.

"If Big Mom says it happened, it happened. My grandmother was a very loyal citizen of the United States and she thought that it was in the best interest of the country not to talk about the event; so she said nothing but that the event shocked grandfather and he never wanted to be Sheriff again after that."

DOCUMENTATION OF THE EVENT

The truth that is out there, the truth more astounding than science fiction, can be found in the archives of the Roswell Historical Society, which holds a little-known document written by George Wilcox' wife, Inez. The couple were always together and made their residence up on the second floor of the jailhouse. During working hours, Inez would come downstairs to the jail and help George around the office, typing and filing reports and assisting in the overall running of operations. There wasn't anything in the jailhouse and Sheriff's Office that George knew that Inez was not cognizant of.

UFO investigator and correspondent Anthony Bragalia writes, "Inez had thought enough about the crash incident to commit some of the details about it to print that her husband could not. The fact that she did so shows that the incident had a lasting impact on her, and that Roswell was indeed discussed (and even documented in a memoir) 'before all the hoopla' with the publiction of the many Roswell books of the early 1990s."

Inez Wilcox' narrative, titled "Four Years in the County Jail," tells the reader what life was like for a law enforcement officer and his wife in the rural American West. Inez thought that one day the memoir might be published in a major circulation magazine like the *Reader's Digest*. In this document, she makes a somewhat cryptic mention about the flying saucer crash, which reads in part:

"One day a rancher north of town brought in what he called a flying saucer. There had been many reports all over the United States by people who claimed they had seen a flying saucer. The ruors were in many variationd: The saucer was from a different planet, and the people flying it were looking down on us. The Germans had invented this strange contraption, a formidable weapon…. Since no one had seen a flying saucer (up close), Mr. Wilcox called Headquarters at Walker Air Force Base (formerly RAAF) and reported the find. Before he hung up the telephone almost, an officer walked in. He quickly loaded the object into a truck and that was the last glimpse that any one had of it.

"Simultaneously, the telephone began to ring, long distance calls from newspapers in New York, England, France and from government officials, military officials, and the calls kept up for 24 hours straight. They would talk to no one but the Sheriff. However, the officer who picked up the suspicious looking saucer admonished Mr. Wilcox to tell as little as possible about it and refer all calls to the base--- A secret well-kept."

And as we have noted previously, George and Inez' two daughters and their granddaughter have affirmed that Inez did, indeed, know a lot more about the UFO crash than what she penned in the document up on a shelf in the Roswell Historical Society's archival section. "Before Mother died at the age of 93," her daughter Phyllis remarked, "she put a short description of what happened in 1947 on paper, which I suspect she wrote before talking to us about the event. Possibly she was still afraid to talk, but even more concerned that the story would be lost."

Two Deputy Sheriffs Clammed Up

Sheriff Wilcox only had two deputies, B. A. "Bernie" Clark and Tommy Thompson; and these deputies were implicated in the UFO crash cover-up by several Roswell townsfolk. Everyone knew that the deputies had been dispatched to the crash site and saw a strange, burned-out and blackened area cordoned off by military personnel from RAAF.

Deputy Clark would only say that he took the initial report from the rancher Mack Brazel concerning the debris that he had discovered out on the range, but always declared that, "There was little substane about the matter." He also remained tight-lipped about the event with his two sons, Gene and Charles Clark, even though they couldn't help being aware that he was out at the crash site on that fateful day.

And Deputy Thompson was always dodging questions about the incident from famiy and inquiring researchers. Thompson was particularly concerned about his fate, seeing that Wilcox' life was in a shambles after getting involved with the case. Not really sure if he was merely jesting, Thompson would tell people asking him about the crash, "I don't want to get shot!" or simply declare, "I wasn't in the office that day," and leave it at that. As to his boss, Sheriff Wilcox, Thompson noted that after the flying saucer episode, "His career was finished, destroyed, and in fact, Wilcox never did seek or run for County Sheriff again."

SHERIFF WILCOX' INTERACTIONS WITH ROSWELL RESIDENTS

Ruben Anaya, a resident of Roswell, New Mexico in 1947, was a staunch Democrat ever since Franklin Delano Roosevelt first ran for President back in 1932. At the time of the Roswell UFO crash, Anaya was a friend of the New Mexico Democrat Lieutenant Governor Joseph Montoya (1915-1978), serving as his chuaffeur during Montoya's reelection campagin. In the early 1990s, Anaya told Roswell UFO researchers that he had driven Montoya out to the RAAF right after news of a crashed flying saucer made the headlines in the *Roswell Daily Record*. When Montoya's visit to the base was concluded, Anaya and two of his brothers were waiting to pick the Lieutenant Governor up and return him back to the hotel where he was lodging.

Per Anaya, as soon as he opened his car door for the Lieutenant Governor to step get in, he couldn't wait and immediately began to tell his brothers all about "extra-terrestrial beings in the base hangar, and that their craft had crashed in the desert." But after dropping the Liutenant Governor back at the hotel, and driving back to their home, the Anaya brothers were met by Sheriff George Wilcox standing out in their front yard. Wondering what the Sheriff wanted, they walked over to greet him. It soon became obvious, however, that Sheriff Wilcox wasn't there to make a social call. Wilcox explained that, "This is a warning. I'm here under the dircction of the military. I know you were out to the base earlier and I want to make this perfectly clear; you are not to say anything about anythig that Lieutenant Governor Montoya had told you about what was going on at the base."

And then there is the testimony of Glenn Dennis, the mortician at the Ballard Funeral Home in Roswell at the time of the UFO crash. Dennis maintains that he was told by a nurse that she had witnessed the corpse of an extraterrestrial at the base hospital. This inspired Dennis to go out to the base hospital and check on the veracity of this alleged "extraterrestrial corpse" being on the premises. But sometime after Dennis returned from the base hospital to his Roswell residence, he discov-ered that his father had been met by Sheriff George A. Wilcox, who declared that, "Despite our friendship, I must state that this visit is not going to be a friendly one. Your son must never speak about anythging that he may have, or thinks he may have seen or heard that was unusual at the base. To do so would cause great harm. Please tell Glenn that he is never to discuss the matter, ever."

John A. Price, now 70 years old, a prominent lifelong Roswell resident, a 1972 graduate from Roswell High School, construction worker, and crash researcher, is the author of *Roswell: A Quest for the Truth* (San Diego, California: Truth Seeker Company, Inc, 1997). In 1980, he asked his friend Bob Dennis, Glenn's fraternal twin brother, if he could confirm Glenn's account. Bob told Price that he wasn't anywhere near Roswell at the time of the crash so he could neither confirm or refute his brother's story. "Frankly," noted Bob, "It's Glenn's story to tell." Nevertheless, Bob did state that when he had returned home for a visit with his father later in 1947, his father did make mention that the ever diligent Sheriff George A. Wilcox had come by the house earlier in the summer "madder than Hell," complaining about Glenn. His father inquired of the Sheriff, "Slow down. What kind of trouble has Glenn gotten himself into?" Bob also remarked that Wilcox was accompanied by Tommy Thompson, the Deputy who insisted that he could not say anything about the Roswell crash for fear of "not wanting to get shot."

ON THE CUTTING EDGE OF HISTORY

It's hard to fairly judge Sheriff Wilcox and his deputies for the way in which they handled the Roswell UFO crash. There was no clear precedent set for dealing with such a situation. However, it has become apparent with the passage of time that the UFO event was real and that these law enforcement officials were "spooked" into silence by government operatives, forever to sit on the truth about the greatest secret in the history of the United States, or maybe the world, that being the crash landing of an exploratory craft from another planet.

FEDERAL BUREAU OF INVESTIGATION (FBI) INTEREST IN ROSWELL

The initial Federal Bureau of Investigation (FBI) communication on the incident came in the form of an 8 July 1947 teletype from the Dallas Field Office regarding a "flying disc" resembling a weather balloon discovered near Roswell. Though not concurrently labeled as a "UFO" or "flying saucer," later FBI documents reveal the Bureau was aware of the alleged crash and recovery of alien bodies, as reported in some accounts. There was also a 1950 memo from the Washington Field Office on the arrest of a con-man trying to scam victims using knowledge of the Roswell incident, thus confirming that the FBI was actively gathering information on the event years after it occurred. This documentation demonstrates that while likely skeptical of the extraterrestrial origins of the flying saucers, the FBI displayed an ongoing interest in gathering intelligence on the most famous UFO case in history.[3]

---

[3] Author unstated, "Declassified: What the FBI Knows About UFOs," *New Space Economy*, 5 February 2024, Declassified: <u>What the FBI Knows About UFOs | New Space Economy,</u> (Accessed 21 July 2025).

POLICE UFO ENCOUNTERS 1947-1959

The significant rise in sightings of flying saucers in the late 1940s and throughout the 1950s by the civilian population resulted in increased reporting and protective responsibilities by law enforcement officials everywhere. Art source: *Beyond Reality Magazine*, Nanuet, New York

Most every ufologist will concur that police officers are among the best trained observers that you will ever come across insofar as they are trained to observe, record and investigate anything suspicious or unusual while on their beat, collecting every detail that might be crucial in the written report that they are all required to submit. Carrying out patrols on a daily and nightly basis, officers of the law have been witnesses to some of the most amazing UFO sightings ever reported. Some have even been caught up in encounters with the UFO occupants.

George Adamski (1891-1965), first of the modern contactees. See http:// ufoarchives.blogspot.com/2015/07/marc-hallet-critical-appraisal-of.html.

INTENSIFICATION OF FLYING SAUCER ACTIVITY FOLLOWING WORLD WAR II

George Adamski (1891-1965), brought over from Poland by his parents at the age of two, and a distinguished U.S. Army veteran, became the most well-known of the contactees after he revealed the details of his encounter with Orthon, an androgynous pilot of a Venusian scout craft near Desert Center, California, on the afternoon of 20 November 1952, in plain view of six witnesses who signed affidavits to that effect.[4]

Orthon informed Adamski that beings from Venus and other planets, not dissimilar in appearance to human beings on Earth, were visiting our planet in greater numbers since the end of World War II because they were worried that nuclear bomb tests and the proliferation of weapons of mass destruction, to include their delivery systems, might radiate or even destroy our world, resulting in the spread of such deadly radiation into space, and the contamination of the other planets in our solar system, or perhaps knocking these orbs out of their orbital positions.

Orthon further explained that many others throughout the world in all walks of life were being contacted by friendly extraterrestrials to help spread this message of peace. Adamski, believing that these extraterrestrials aimed to guide and warn humans about the dangers of their militant actions, provided the full details of his initial encounter on the physical plane of existence with Orthon, and the message he received from this alien being, in the pages of his book, co-authored with Sir Desmond Leslie of British royalty, *Flying Saucers Have Landed* (New York, New York: British Book Centre, 1953). The publicity surrounding Adamski and his contact claims attracted the attention of various FBI offices around the country. For a detailed report on the FBI investigations of George Adamski, please see Appendix A.

EARLY POLICE ENCOUNTERS

Because police serve on a local level as first responders to any emergency, they are usually the quickest to arrive on the scene for any distress calls. This would include sightings or more in-depth encounters with UFOs and/or their attending occupants. In 1956, the National Investigations Committee on Aerial Phenomena (NICAP), a non-profit, civilian UFO research organization, was formed in Washington, D.C. The organization endured as the largest such civilian UFO investigative group until 1980, whence it was eventually eclipsed by the Mutual UFO Network (MUFON).

---

[4]   The Federal Bureau of Investigation (FBI) Director J. Edgar Hoover took an active interest in the prominent contactee case of George Adamski. See Appendix B for the details of the FBI's Adamski investigation.

For most of NICAP's existence, it was directed by the able military aviator and journalist, Retired Marine Corps Major Donald E. Keyhoe. Under Keyhoe's strong guidance, qualified field investigators were mustered from every state and territory of the United States, even retrieving and checking out the older reports as best they could. In the process of accomplishing this task, countless police UFO reports were accumulated and added to NICAP's data base. Following the dissolution of NICAP, however, all catalogued UFO reports were transferred to the headquarters of the Center for UFO Studies (CUFOS) in Evanston, Illinois, immediately to the north of Chicago, an organization founded by Dr. J. Allen Hynek, a former Air Force Project Bluebook scientific consultant for over twenty years and then astronomy professor at Northwestern University in Evanston.

Many thanks are extended to Michael M. Deschamps, Director of the Northern Ontario UFO Research and Study (NOUFORS) of Sudbury, Ontario, Canada, for his retrieval and summation that you find below of some of the more notable reports of law enforcement encounters in those crucial years from the history of ufology, the late 1940s through the decade of the 1950s.

1947

4 July: Patrolman Kenneth A. McDowell of Portland, Oregon, sights five discs in an up- and-down oscillation.

7 July: Patrolmen Evan Davis and Stan Johnson of Tacoma, Washington, observe three spinning objects with an undiscernible shape emitting sparks and seemingly drawing them back in while hovering and then abruptly changing direction.

1948

7 January: Kentucky State Police in the vicinity of Godman Air Force Base report seeing a huge, round UFO. This was on the same day that Air Force Captain Charles Mantell, scrambled from Godman Air Force Base, crashed his jet in pursuit of a UFO.

1952

28 July: State Patrolmen Charles Longstreet and Norman Mellis in Shelby County, Indiana, view a star-like UFO "move up and down, and back and forth, and sometimes hover."

28 August: Six officers from Atlanta, Georgia, most notably Patrolmen M. J. Spears and A. L. Elsberry, filed reports of a UFO changing color. Spears and Elsberry remarked that, "Every so often it would sprout a red flamed trail; then it would move up and down…. It turned a flip a couple of times."

22 September: Fairfax County, Virginia, Police Sergeant Wall and Police Privates Dunn, Burke and Eherill, encounter one to four UFOs maneuvering in and out of their patrol sectors. Dunn observed three to four at one time, declaring that "Each object looked like a white ball of fire coming out of the clouds…. They would come and go. It was like tag." Burke thought the encounter very strange: "One would pop out here, there…. Weird…. Weird indeed."

1953

11-13 September: Chiloquin, Oregon, Police Chief Lew Jones reported "top-like UFOs, seen by many citizens over three nights," including himself. Jones watched the UFOs through a pair of binoculars, attesting that the UFOs were "top-shaped" with lights running along their fuselages.

1955

2 November: Deputy Sheriff A. H. Perkins and Patrolman C. F. Bell of Williston, Florida, witnessed UFOs also seen by over a dozen area residents. Perkins observed the UFOs on two separate occasions, while Bell saw six oval-shaped UFOs moving in spurts, but all the while feeling a "stinging heat."

1956

24-25 November: On the outskirts of Rapid City, South Dakota, Sheriff Glen Best and State Patrolman C. D. Erikson chased a UFO emitting a steady green light and flashing a red light. The UFO occasionally beamed a strong white light skyward. This encounter took place amid a huge UFO flap with widespread sightings taking place over and in the vicinity of Ellsworth Air Force Base, located about ten miles to the northeast of Rapid City. Many Air Force pilots from Ellsworth reported UFOs while in the air, and there were rumors of these reports' verifications coming from radar contact at the base's flight tower.

1957

2 November: In Levelland, Texas, Sheriff Weir Clem and Deputy Pat McCullough witnessed a bright, red-elliptical UFO, also seen by many other of the townsfolk.

4 November: In Elmwood Park, Illinois, Officers Joseph Lukasek, Clifford Schau and Daniel DeGiovanni observed a round, reddish-object hovering over the town's cemetery. Elmwood Park residents were quite upset by all the commotion, but calmed down with the arrival of the police. Perhaps the arrival of two cruisers with their lights flashing and sirens blaring, provided an impetus for the object to clear the cemetery, whence it purportedly fell away, drifting off into the horizon.

6 November: State Policemen Calvin Showers and John Matulis of Danville, Illinois, watched a brilliant white light change to an alternating amber and then to an orange color for about twenty minutes. They wanted to radio their report in to headquarters, but so long as the UFO remained in view, their radio failed them.

10 November: The appearance of an elongated, cigar-shaped UFO with red and white lights along its fuselage caused Hammond, Indiana, policemen Captain Dennis Becky and Officers Charles Moore, Charles Mauder and Steven Betusak to pursue the object in two patrol cars up to the city limits, whence the craft sped quickly out of sight. While in pursuit of the UFO, the radios in the two cruisers were overcome with static, inhibiting communications. As soon as the UFO sped away, however, the radio signals returned to normal. Throughout November of 1957, there was a spate of UFO sightings across the Midwest, with countless reports of aerial phenomena being called in to police stations with officers being dispatched to investigate.

1958

9 April: Patrolman R. Gordon of Newport Beach, California, reported two flat objects with rows of six flashing lights on their leading edge being observed low above the ocean with their respective light arrays being reflected in the water beneath them. The two UFOs executed sharp turns and then shot out over the Pacific Ocean, fading quickly out of sight.

24 August: Patrolmen Richard Schulz and Richard McCabe of Westwood, New Jersey, reported a glowing orange, circular UFO hovering over the downtown area. It was moving rapidly towards the east and was out of sight within seconds.

12 October: In Aurora, Illinois, Patrolmen William Hornyan and Jack Adams, along with about a dozen civilian witnesses, watched several UFOs in the distance scatter across the sky in multiple directions.

1959

3 April: Retired U.S. Treasury Enforcement Officer and former Coast Guard Lieutenant John F. Wilmeth of Ocoee, Florida, observed a large greenish-yellow light ascending above nearby Lake Apopka, to the northwest of the Greater Orlando area, with this unusual light being reflected in the water underneath. The object then seemed to descend into the waters and then rise again, hovering for about 30 seconds before ascending quickly and zipping out of sight. Here is a case of a traditional UFO exhibiting the characteristics of an unidentified submarine object (USO).

POLICE DETECTIVE'S LETTER TO NEWLY CREATED "PROJECT BLUEBOOK"

Mansfield, Ohio, Police Detective John E. Steel filed one of the first UFO reports on record with Project Bluebook at Wright-Patterson Air Force Base in Dayton, Ohio. Drawing source: Alamy

John E. Steel was a detective with the Mansfield, Ohio, Police Department who after reading an article in the April 1952 issue of *Life Magazine* (New York City, New York) about the establishment of an ongoing, systematic study of UFOs by the Air Force in March 1952, codenamed Project Blue Book and headquartered at Wright-Patterson Air Force Base in Dayton, Ohio, felt inspired to write a letter to the investigative body's director, Captain Edward J. Ruppelt, about his own UFO encounter that took place about two years prior (in the spring of 1950), at approximately 10 p.m.:

Date: 7 April 1952
Letter to: Commanding Officer, Air Technical Intelligence Center, Wright-Patterson Air Force Base, Dayton, Ohio
From: John E. Steel, Detective Bureau, Police Department, Mansfield, Ohio
Captain Ruppelt:

In concurrence with the implied request incorporated in the April 1952 *Life Magazine* article to report to your office any unidentified aircraft sighted in the sky, I respectfully submit the following for your consideration:

Approximately two years ago, my wife and I attended an outdoor theatre situated about four miles northeast of Mansfield, Ohio, on State Route 42. We entered this theatre after the show had started and consequently left before the last show was out. As we were driving out of the theatre, in a southwest direction to the highway, my wife pointed out the right front window of the car and called my attention to two large red lights in the sky and remarked that she had never noticed any radio tower I that particular direction before. I looked to where she directed and noticed what appeared to be red lights such as are installed atop radio towers and other high installations. I realized that the lights were evidently out of place because when we passed this area on our way to the theatre, there was no installation in that locality. I told my wife to watch the lights until I got out onto the highway; and at the same time, I looked at my watch and noted that the time was exactly 2200 hours.

As I turned right onto the highway and headed for Mansfield, I noticed that the lights were to the left of the highway. I drove approximately four-tenths of a mile and as I approached these lights, my wife and I saw what appeared to be a large spot light, about the size of the lens on anti-aircraft lights, flash on with the beam directed at the ground, directly under the lights above. This beam was visible for only the fraction of a second; and the light was intense and about the same color as bright daylight on a clear summer day, with the Sun directly overhead. There was absolutely no sign of reflection or refraction from this light, and the stubbled farmer's field (cleared of vegetation) was revealed completely, without shadow and within the scope of the light.

I immediately stopped my car and got out and walked to the rear of the car in order to get a better view of whatever the object of our curiosity might be; and by being away from the light of my headlights, I was able to make out a shape in the sky. The night was clear and a certain amount of natural light existed, and I saw what appeared to be the hull or bottom of the cabin of a large blimp. The reason for this association is that I have seen them on numerous occasions at night over Mansfield, as they came in from Akron, Ohio (Goodyear blimps). This hull or craft was a dark gray in color, and I am positive that there was no blimp or gas bag above what appeared to be the hull. This craft, as nearly as I could estimate, was about one hundred feet off the ground and possibly seventy yards to one hundred yards to the left of the highway, directly over a stubbled field. At this time, I noticed that the red lights mentioned above looked exactly like the tail lights on the new Cadillac automobiles; and these lights were situated at either the stem or stern of the craft.

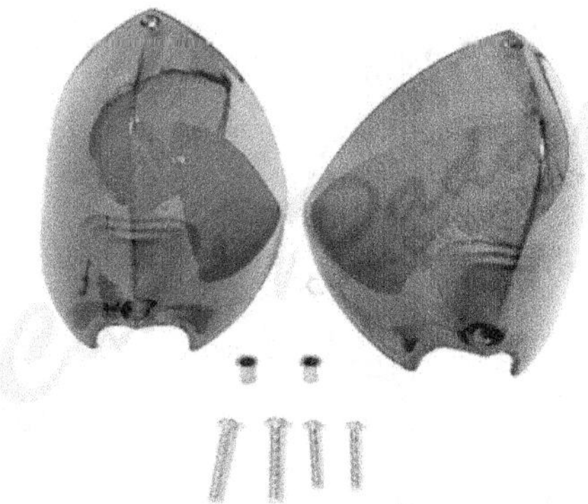

The two UFOs had the appearance/shape of the 1951-1953 Cadillac tail lights depicted above. Cadillac tail assembly photo from caddydaddy.com.

This craft was extremely motionless and silent. At this time, there was absolutely no other vehicles on the highway; and I could see and hear perfectly. As I was standing there trying to figure the thing out, the craft suddenly took off in a southeast direction at an unheard-of rate of speed. There was no acceleration. It was a case of full speed from a dead stop. I watched the craft from the time it started up until it disappeared over the horizon, approximately eight to ten miles away; and the lapsed time was not more than three seconds, by my watch. I also noticed that there was absolutely no exhaust flash nor any sound from the craft.

May I state that my reason for being so sure of the above is that in combat overseas during World War II, it was my duty over a period of months to report the direction, approximate height, speed and type of aircraft flying over our area, wherever we may be.

After the craft had gone out of sight, I immediately drove to the Mansfield Airport, base of the 164th Fighter Squadron, Ohio National Guard, where I contacted one Major Line and related the above to him. The major took some notes and listened to my account of the incident and stated that he would take care of it. I assumed that to date, no consideration was due my account; but since reading the above-mentioned *Life* captioned-article, I feel it is my duty to make sure that you have been advised of the above.

In conclusion, may I again state that the above is submitted for your consideration, and I stand ready to be of any service possible.

—**John E. Steel**

Author's comments: The above-communication from Police Detective John E. Steel comes from the "Letters to the Air Force UFO Files" of former Civil Defense Ground Observers Corps member Loren E. Gross of Richmond, California, who, in turn, obtained it from declassified Air Force documents then extant in 1953.

HONORABLY DISCHARGED from the Richmond Ground Observer Corps was Loren Gross, left, son of Mr. and Mrs. J. L. Gross of 5101 Esmond avenue. Gross and several others were discharged through an Air Force order which established a minimum age limit. Lieutenant Richard B. Moon of the Oakland Filter Center presented the under-age ground observers with their discharges. W. C. Kates is post supervisor of the Corps. — Independent Pho'

As an historical note, Project Bluebook replaced the two prior Air Force investigative groups focused on unidentified aerial phenomena, these being Project Sign, established in 1947, followed by Project Grudge in 1949. Project Bluebook was terminated by the Air Force on 17 December 1969 upon the recommendation of the United States government-contracted *Scientific Study of UFOs* (New York City, New York: New York Times/Bantam Books, 1969), carried out by the University of Colorado at Boulder (1966-1968), then directed by the prominent nuclear physicist Dr. Edward U. Condon (1902-1974).

BEYOND ROSWELL: SERGEANT LONNIE ZAMORA AND THE NEW MEXICO FLYING SAUCER FLAP OF 1963-1964

Air Force brass dispatched Dr. J. Allen Hynek of Northwestern University in Evanston, Illinois, to investigate the great New Mexico flying saucer flap of 1964 and calm public fears, in the process. See *https://secure.action.news/watch?v=GjByxf7XOU0*.

"UFOs Pose No Threat"

At the close of 1963, the United States Air Force Project Bluebook investigative personnel had checked out 8,128 reported cases of unidentified flying objects (UFOs) in the United States. This special Air Force program was established 16 years prior for the express purpose of determining whether the UFOs represented some threat to our national security. Of these reports, 7.7 percent of the cases remained classified as "unidentified." The other 92.3 percent of the objects reported turned out to be misinterpretations of celestial or natural phenomena, conventional aircraft or aerospace vehicles seen under unusual atmospheric conditions or outright hoaxes.

From the start of 1964 and through the following six months, however, there was an intensification of UFO activity over the state of New Mexico. The Air Force's leading civilian consultant was the chief astronomer at Northwestern University's Dearborn Observatory, Dr. J. Allen Hynek. For the most part, Dr. Hynek would stay behind on Northwestern's Chicago, Illinois, campus and just wait for the investigative team to bring in all the amassed data for correlation. Nevertheless, the epidemic of strange sightings over New Mexico skies required that the Air Force brass dispatch Dr. Hynek to the state, as one of their "big guns," to calm down the local populace and find out what was really happening with the UFOs.

The first case that Dr. Hynek investigated in New Mexico, the "Land of Enchantment," involved a highway patrolman's encounter with an egg-shaped UFO that landed a little distance off the main state route in the vicinity of his hometown of Socorro. The officer, Sergeant Lonnie Zamora, was just about to wrap it up for the day. It was 5:45 p.m. on the evening of 24 April 1964; and his shift was about to end in 15 minutes. Out of the blue, a speeder raced by Zamora's position, moving like a "bat out of hell." The patrolman was about to chase the speeder when suddenly there was a loud explosion coming from the rear. Also, when Lonnie Zamora heard the fierce clapping noise, he turned around just in time to catch sight of an eerie light blue flash of light that washed over him, his patrol car and the surrounding desert shrubbery.

Zamora followed in his patrol car a dirt path to a small shack about 200 feet back from the highway, whence the blue flash and the explosion emanated. That's when he spotted the source of all the commotion, a shiny, ovular object descending from the sky with a smokeless blue and orange flame emitting from its underside.

The officer described the object as resembling, "a car turned upside down.... standing on its radiator or trunk." At this point, Zamora got out of his vehicle and started to approach the now landed object to within 100 feet on foot. Two personages in white coveralls had disembarked from the strange object. "One of these persons," noted the highway patrolman, "seemed to turn and look straight at my car and seemed startled- seemed to quickly jump somewhat."

Patrolman Zamora described the UFO occupants as "normal in shape, but possibly they were small adults or large kids." The officer radioed for backup but continued to keep his distance from the object and the beings that descended from it. The oval-shaped UFO had no visible windows or even the seams for a doorway. It sat upon girder-like legs. The craft was marked, however, with a red insignia that was about two-an-a-half feet wide. The UFO occupants, on the other hand, were not going to remain in the area for long insofar as the armed patrolman was there observing their activities. In the next five minutes, the two aliens quickly terminated their activities, got back into their craft, and took off. Zamora witnessed the UFO quickly ascend and then move over a mountain in the distance, whence it quickly sped out of sight, but not out of mind. Just a few minutes after the aliens' departure, fellow officer Sergeant Sam Chavez of the New Mexico State Police arrived at the scene in response to Zamora's radio call for backup. Officer Chavez, while he did not see the object, did observe the still-smoldering brush the UFO had landed and taken off. He also noted four burn marks and four V-shaped depressions pushed into the ground where the object had rested. These impressions were between one and two inches deep and each one measured eighteen inches in length.

One of the chief skeptics of the era, Dr. Philip J. Klass, the editor of *Aviation and Space Technology* magazine, opined that Zamora had simply made up the whole story to increase tourism in the area. However, in a report submitted to the Central Intelligence Agency by the then director of the Air Force's Project Bluebook, Major Hector Quintanilla, the highest military authority on the UFO phenomenon declared that, "There is no doubt that Lonnie Zamora saw an object which left quite an impression on him. There is also no question about Zamora's reliability. He is a serious officer, a pillar of his church, and a man well-versed in recognizing airborne vehicles in this area. He was puzzled by what he saw, and frankly, so are we." Keep in mind that the Bluebook director came to these conclusions based on the field research conducted by Dr. J. Allen Hynek on his behalf.

Sergeant Lonnie Zamora witnesses landing and takeoff of oval-shaped UFO, to include its occupants. The officer also noted a bright red inscription on the side of the alien object. See *https://i.ytimg.com/vi/ZUA_etT1GVI/hqdefault.jpg*.

The revelation of Dr. Hynek's involvement in the Zamora case was leaked in the 30 April 1964 edition of the *News-Sun* newspaper of Hobbs, New Mexico. Despite the official pronouncements by Project Bluebook personnel that there was no evidence linking UFOs to extraterrestrial spaceships, the Air Force's overwhelming interest in this Socorro, New Mexico, UFO landing incident suggested otherwise. The "genie was out of the bottle," so to speak, and getting him back in was not going to be an easy task.

LIFE ON ANOTHER PLANET FEASIBLE

Clearly, the nation, if not the entire world, was electrified by Sergeant Zamora's account of a UFO landing, complete with a sighting of occupants. In the very day following the news of Hynek's arrival in New Mexico to investigate the Socorro event, an article appeared in the Salt Lake City, Utah, *Deseret News and Telegram* newspaper titled, "Life on Other Planet, Researcher Claims: Let's Contact Them,

Meet Told." Remarks made by Dr. Bernard M. Oliver, the vice president in charge of research and development at the Hewlett-Packard Company, at a three-day regional conference of the Institute of Electrical and Electronics Engineers (IEEE) held in downtown Salt Lake City's Hotel Utah, affirmed the feasibility of intelligent life existing on another planet.

"Man is not alone in the universe," said Dr. Oliver, adding that, "If we make the effort, we can contact other life. Mankind now has the capability to contact life on other planets."

Sergeant Zamora's New Mexico desert encounter with unusual beings emerging from a UFO was certainly causing many to reconsider the extraterrestrial hypothesis. In Dr. Oliver's opinion, the universe was abounding with life. To the crowd of electrical engineers, he offered the belief that life is common in the universe; and that, "The density of life is such that there are, no doubt, several populations within the present radio range." Dr. Oliver, when asked why there had been no contacts with life of any significance on these other nearby worlds, speculated that it was "because no real, concerted effort has been made to do so."

Dr. Oliver felt that, "Such a contact would have as profound an impact on our world culture as did the voyage of Columbus on the culture of the Old World. With our present sending and receiving equipment, our chances of contacting other intelligent civilizations are really quite high." He mused that the cost of such a program would be negligible, at least when compared with the overall impact it would have. Dr. Oliver was the featured speaker during the banquet session of the IEEE, as well as the recipient of a research award. Also recognized during the same session was Dr. Obed C. Haycock, director of the University of Utah Upper Air Research Laboratory, for his contributions to research on the upper atmosphere and to engineering education. Not surprisingly, Dr. Haycock's considered opinions about extraterrestrial life coincided with Dr. Oliver's.

"Stay Away from All UFOs!"

In the weeks before and after Sergeant Lonnie Zamora's close encounter, sightings of UFOs all over the Land of Enchantment had risen to a fever pitch. The *New Mexican* newspaper of Santa Fe, New Mexico, dated 29 April 1964, reported a sorry and unusual incident at an Albuquerque elementary school, where a young girl was out on the playground at recess when an egg-shaped UFO swooped down over the swing sets. The lass was standing right under the object; and while looking up at it, suffered burns on her face and the exposed portion of her arms. Upon hearing about this incident, the Santa Fe, New Mexico, police chief, A. B. Martinez, decided to issue a warning to all students and residents of his city to, "Stay away from any mysterious objects." The top law enforcement official added that, "I don't know what these objects really are; but if any are sighted by local residents, they should be treated with respect and caution until more information as to their identity is available."

Strange Occurrences Afoot in New Mexico

While the attention of the United States was focused on New Mexico because of this flying saucer flap and particularly Lonnie Zamora's amazing encounter, news of yet another alien contact case emerged in the pages of the 1 May 1964, Albuquerque, New Mexico, *Journal* newspaper. Apolinar A. Villa, Jr. (1916-1982), who described himself as "just an ordinary working man- just a mechanic," was puzzled as to why the extraterrestrials chose to contact him and establish direct communications. "They said there was a purpose," Villa told *Journal* reporter Martin Paskind, adding that, "What it is, I don't know."

Apolinar Villa's friends just call him "Paul." They don't know what to think about his claims, however, that he has been visited by extraterrestrials at least five times over the past five years; that's once a year on average. On several occasions, he even enjoyed the opportunity of talking to the alien visitors; and he was even allowed to take pictures of the flying saucer that brought them to our planet. Following one close encounter of the third kind, Villa filled up an entire roll of film with Kodacolor photos of the aliens' spacecraft.

At the time that reporter Paskind interviewed Villa about his close encounters, the still relatively unknown contactee was 47 years old and lived with his son and daughter-in-law in a trailer behind 601 Niagara Avenue in the northeast section of Albuquerque. Born in Tijeras, New Mexico, the young Villa attended Longfellow Elementary School and Lincoln Junior High School. He dropped out of high school in his freshman year to work in his family's gas station and garage. After a few years, Villa then enlisted in the Army Air Force, where he served as a mechanic in a motor pool on a base in California. Receiving an honorable discharge, Villa stayed out on the West Coast for a couple of years, securing a job with the Los Angeles Department of Power and Water, before returning home to New Mexico where he began working as a mechanic for N. C. Ribble and Company, where has been employed ever since.

Villa showed the reporter some of the photos of the flying saucer. "The pictures are authentic," the mechanic asserted, adding that, "They're the real thing."

The mechanic told Paskind that there were a lot of things he just could not talk about because he did not think that anybody would believe him. For example, Villa talked about an encounter with the aliens that allegedly took place on 16 June 1963. From 2:30 to 4:00 p.m. on that day, the contactee supposedly conversed with extraterrestrial men and women aboard their spacecraft that was hovering above the New Mexico desert a few miles to the northwest of Albuquerque. The space people allowed Villa to bring his Japanese camera along with him in order to take some clear photographs of their interplanetary conveyance.

**Original photo of flying saucer taken by Paul Villa on 16 June
1963 in area to immediate northwest of Albuquerque, New Mexico.
Photo from files of Gabriel Green, President of Amalgamated
Flying Saucer Clubs of America, Yucca Valley, California.**

Onboard the flying saucer, Villa's extraterrestrial friends explained to him that while they were not gods or even superhuman, they were generally superior to our species in physical qualities and quantity of knowledge. The UFO crew members also informed him about coming volcanic activity along certain ridges in the Pacific Ocean's so-called Ring of Fire and commented on the growing economic and military power of the People's Republic of China, of which they warned that wise politicians should not ignore. It seemed to Villa that the flying saucer occupants had some inkling of future events. After his conversation with the aliens, Villa took a rather fatalistic attitude, declaring that he had come to learn that, "We can't get away from what God has decreed for us. Even they (the extraterrestrials) know that there is a Super Intelligence that governs the universe and everything in it."

Villa sighted his first UFO in 1953 when he was working out on the West Coast with the utilities company. While he was looking up at the object, he was approached from behind by an androgynous being in a blue jumpsuit with long, blonde hair. The being tapped the utility worker on his right shoulder. Startled, Villa turned to see who it was and what was wanted. "Now you know that the flying saucers are real," is all that the mysterious entity said before disappearing in a glint of light. When he first moved back to New Mexico and settled in Albuquerque, he lived at 4187 Edith St., on the northeast side. On two occasions, UFOs hovered directly over his home. On the second pass over his home, the roof caught fire from the intense radiation emitted from the underside of the flying saucer. And once on his way back from attending a rodeo in Lindrith, New Mexico, the mechanic came across a disc-shaped UFO that he estimated to be about 900 feet in diameter. This was by far the largest object that Villa had observed. In second place in this category was a saucer viewed outside Peralta, New Mexico, that he estimated to be about 160 feet in diameter. This craft landed; and from it stepped several crew members. In their blue jumpsuits they all had an androgynous appearance, so Villa could make no determination as to their sexes. Their uniforms displayed no rank; but the one who spoke to Villa emitted an aura of authority and seemed to be in charge. The being explained that they had just returned from an important mission in a distant elliptical galaxy visible from Earth in the Coma Berenices star cluster and were on their way home to a neighboring planet in our own solar system. The smaller UFOs were all like the typical flying saucer so commonly reported, about 50 feet in diameter and sometimes referred to in ufology circles as scoutcraft. Over the years, and through his physical and telepathic communications with the extraterrestrials, Villa gradually acquired fragmentary knowledge of the star people and their operations on Earth.

Conversation with a Master

On one occasion, Villa asked the extraterrestrials why evidence of their civilization in our solar system had not been detected, now that the National Aeronautics and Space Administration (NASA) has sent probes to some of the nearer planets. "Paul, we are about two million years more advanced than the highest pinnacles of your civilization on Earth; therefore, we understand your inadequacy. Even if you were to land astronauts on our planet, there would be scarce evidence for our civilization. In a thousand years, humans from Earth may begin to reach out and meet some of us; but it will take thousands more before you can approach our civilization on something like equal terms. To you of Earth, our planet is nothing more than a world of dreams. While it has the texture of reality, it is quite tenuous. We can modify its presentation at will in terms of color, quality or even shape. We live just outside your own space-time continuum. We can take you to realms of the universe that you have not even imagined and even to parts of it where life is just beginning to form and set out on the path of evolutionary progress. The best way I can put this is that we exist at a slightly higher vibrational frequency than you of Earth."

"From your description, it seems like you are gods and live in Heaven," remarked Paul Villa.

"I wouldn't go that far, Paul," replied his extraterrestrial contact. "We were humans much like yourselves, once upon a time; but we went on to master the subtleties of the inner dimensions. One day you will reach the point of cosmic evolution where we are now, provided you don't go the way of the dinosaurs and bring about your own extinction through warfare or the disregard of your natural environment."

"OK, so what brings you to New Mexico, if I might ask?" queried Villa.

Our other-worldly visitor retorted that, "We star people are interested in New Mexico because of a magnetic fault in Farmington…. Our ships travel along magnetic lines. They put a lot of stress on New Mexico and parts of Arizona and Utah. In fact, one of our ships crashed in 1948 near this area when the magnetic lines were warped by atomic testing out in the Nevada desert. The commander of our Moon base was dispatched to see what she could find out and do something about it."

Bad Luck

Like the words of a country music song, "If it weren't for bad luck, I'd have no luck at all," Paul Villa's life was not an easy one. Many of his acquaintances gave up on him altogether, at best thinking he was eccentric and at worse, thinking him insane. He suffered a great steak of misfortune. By the time of the interview, his home burned down to the ground and he didn't have fire insurance. He accidentally shot himself in the arm during a hunting trip; and he had to file for bankruptcy. For a while, Villa wondered if the extraterrestrials were working some sort of mischief in his life, maybe for something that he should not have said, or something that he did to displease them. But then he mused, "No, they were a very friendly sort of people. Their opinion is not that we are good or bad; but they are not about to save us from ourselves." This caused me to think that such, I suppose, are the travails awaiting most of us who inhabit this entropic universe.

Villa's Assertions Vindicated

News of the New Mexico flap, along with the close encounters of Zamora and Villa, while becoming the butt of jokes in many quarters of the United States, where certainly being taken with a higher degree of gravitas in the United Kingdom. UFOs were always a hot topic on the airwaves of radio and television news programming of the British Broadcasting Company (BBC). Many of the contactees like Howard Menger of New Jersey and Paul Villa in New Mexico were claiming that the flying saucers originated from bases on planets in our own solar system. At the same time, spokespersons for NASA were adamant in pressing their claim that conditions on planets like Venus or Mars were just too unlike those on Earth to support any kind of life, at least as "we know it."

On 28 April 1964, however, the BBC featured an interview with Professor H. Bruck, the Scottish Astronomer Royal, who was attending a conference of the Royal Astronomical Society in Edinburgh and made time to drop into the BBC studios there in the evening to discuss the timely subject of the existence of intelligent life on other planets. When asked about intelligent life in other solar systems, or even other galaxies, Professor Bruck did not dispute that it probably exists, but argued that if the current laws of physics are correct, it would take many of our lifetimes for a spaceship to reach Earth if it were emanating from such a far point. On the other hand, the question about life in our own solar system brought the quite unexpected answer that not only does it exist, but that Venus and Mars are likely to have human populations and that, "It is very likely that they are visiting us now." A complete transcript of the program was published in the May-June 1964 edition of *Spacelink*, the official organ of the Isle of Wight UFO Investigation Society in the United Kingdom.

Robert C. Gribble, the director of the Aerial Phenomena Research Group (APRG) in Seattle, Washington, of which I (Dr. R. A. Keller) was a member at the time, lamented that space researchers in the United States were not as forthcoming as their counterparts on the "other side of the pond," so to speak. Gribble commented that, "It is hoped that other astronomers, in professional and amateur circles, will take note of this enlightened viewpoint, publicly expressed by the Scottish Astronomer Royal."

OHIO AS THE LOCUS OF UFO ACTIVITY AND THE 1966 FLYING SAUCER POLICE CHASE

Ohio has long been considered a locus for UFO activity over the United States. Leonard Stringfield of Cincinnati (1920-1994), when he was not working as the advertising manager for Du Bois Chemicals, served as the director for his home town's Unidentified Flying Object Society, back in the late 1950s and early 1960s. Stringfield first became interested in ufology in 1945. At that time, he was on active duty in the Army Air Corps, the predecessor of the now independent branch of the armed forces, the United States Air Force, when he spotted a formation of flying saucers from the window of a bomber.

As World War II had ended slightly before this sighting, he initially thought that the elusive UFOs might be some kind of Soviet experimental aircraft. With the intent of doing his part to stem the red peril, Springfield continued to serve as a spotter for the Air Defense Command. In that capacity, the Cincinnati pioneer ufologist discovered that many more service members and veterans had sighted these objects both during the war and after.

By 1960, however, Stringfield began to reassess his Soviet origin hypothesis. The technology exhibited by the UFOs evidenced a science far beyond anything of this world. In the Saturday, 4 June 1960 edition of the Cincinnati *Post and Times Star*, the UFO Society director opined that, "I believe the UFOs are from outer space and that they are controlled by intelligent beings who are observing the Earth." He added that, "I don't believe there is any hostile intent; but I believe they have been using planets in our solar system for bases, even the Moon. Astronomers for years have observed shifting spots on the Moon."

Stringfield was also held the considered opinion that the United States Air Force's secret files contained evidence, or "near evidence," at the least, bolstering the so-called extraterrestrial hypothesis, i.e. that the flying saucers originated from somewhere in outer space. The ufologist did not think that the Air Force was going to make any disclosures about this anytime soon, however, insofar as government officials were probably afraid that this kind of information, if it were released to the public, would cause mass panic. He also concluded that foreign governments, especially the communist regime in the Soviet Union, also have evidence that UFOs are arriving at our world from other planets but are keeping it secret, for the very same reason and in the interest of their own national security.

It is interesting to note that Stringfield, in the midst of the Cold War at a time when the United States was rushing to close the missile gap and catch up in the space race with the Soviet Union, told the reporter from the Cincinnati newspaper that, "I believe it is time we took the space spotlight away from Russia by opening up secret files on unidentified flying objects. It could be the start of co-operation among all governments of the world."

Perhaps it was wishful thinking on Stringfield's part, but he concluded that, "If all governments would pool their information on UFOs and work in unison on this, it would help to ease world tensions."

See https://www.phantomsandmonsters.com/2014/04/the-1966-ohio-pennsylvania-ufo-police.html for additional information on this amazing encounter. This case was used by Steven Spielberg to model the police pursuit of a UFO scene in his classic movie, *Close Encounters of the Third Kind* (Columbia Pictures, 1977).

"IT HAPPENED IN OHIO…."

Perhaps one of the more interesting UFO cases of all time also took place in Ohio. This involved an encounter with a flying saucer in Ravenna, Ohio, by on duty Portage County Sheriff's deputies Dale F. Spaur, the senior officer, and W. L. "Barney" Neff, the special deputy, around 5:00 a.m. on 17 April 1966. Spaur was driving patrol car number 13, accompanied by Neff in the front seat. The deputies ended up chasing a UFO 86 miles through Ohio and on into Pennsylvania.

It all began under unusual circumstances. While on patrol, the deputies noticed a red and white 1959 Ford sedan parked alongside the road. Naturally, the officers stopped to check it out. The Ford had a strange emblem on its side. There was an inverted triangle with a bolt of lightning in its center, along with an overriding inscription, "Seven Steps to Hell." And in the front and back seats of the automobile, the deputies could see dozens of walkie-talkies and other apparent electronic gear of an undetermined nature.[5]

Suddenly, Spaur heard a humming sound, like a swarm of bees, emanating from behind him. He turned and saw a huge, saucer-shaped craft rising out of the woods. The officer, accustomed to gauging the size of vehicles on the road, estimated that the flying saucer was about 50 feet in diameter and perhaps 15 to 20 feet high. The object had a dome and antenna on top; and the underside gleamed with an intense, purplish-white light.

The officers became transfixed and immobile. The saucer rose to about 150 feet and moved directly above the Ford and the officers standing next to it. Both Spaur and Neff felt a warm, pleasing heat as the object hovered over them. However, the light from the underside of the UFO was so intense that tears were streaming down from the eyes of the deputies. At one point, Spaur felt as if he was regaining mobility, but hesitated to make a move toward the nearby parked patrol car. He thought that it would be wiser to play a wait and see game before taking any abrupt actions.

---

[5]   Bill Moore, "It Happened in Ohio….," *Limbo*, Oklahoma City, Oklahoma, Vol. 1, No. 1, January-February 1971. Paranormal researchers like the late John A. Keel (1930-2009), would attach great significance to the appearance of this unusual Ford sedan with its strange emblem. The design may provide some indication of a supernatural significance to the UFO encounter. –Cosmic Ray

Neff looked over to Spaur, seeking guidance. Spaur nodded his head in the direction of the patrol car. Then the two deputies made a mad dash for their cruiser. The officers jumped in their vehicle and Spaur radioed in, telling headquarters about the UFO. Other reports from local residents were made of the object and these, too, were flooding into the sheriff's office. The dispatcher responded to Spaur's report with the command to "Shoot it!" However, the experienced Spaur reasoned that getting out of his vehicle to fire at the object would be foolhardy and most likely would get him and his partnering deputy killed.

In the interim, the object was now hovering over the patrol car. Back at headquarters, the night sergeant grabbed the microphone from the dispatcher. "Try to find out more about the thing. And if it moves away from there, just chase it," said the sergeant to Spaur. At that, the large saucer drifted slowly away. Spaur followed and then the object picked up some speed. Spaur put his foot on the cruiser's accelerator to keep up with the UFO. He was now driving at a good clip of 100 miles per hour in pursuit of the strange craft.

Whatever intelligence was behind the flying saucer seemed to let Deputy Spaur follow it in on its eastward path, even waiting for the cruiser to catch up at intersections. Once, the object even appeared to have doubled back when Spaur was forced to veer away from the easterly direction. The officers in patrol car number 13 crossed over into the neighboring state of Pennsylvania in their high-speed pursuit. The deputies drove as far as the outskirts of Pittsburgh following the UFO. Only running out of gas prohibited them from continuing the chase.

This UFO case was first investigated by the then Director of the Cleveland Ufology Project (CUP), Earl J. Neff (not related to Deputy W. L. Neff). Earl Neff, however, was the former sketch artist for Eliot Ness of "Untouchables" fame, when Ness served as the Cleveland, Ohio, Safety Commissioner in the 1930s. The CUP Director appreciated the frankness of Sheriff's Deputy Spaur in forthrightly answering all the questions that he put to him about the UFO encounter. Deputy Neff, however, refused to talk about the incident. Apparently, the unfavorable news coverage was creating some problems for him at work and in his home environment. Appendix B details the long-term travails experienced by Deputy Sheriff Spaur due to his more thorough reporting of the UFO encounter.

CUP Director Neff (1902-1993) remarked that other law enforcement officers on duty that morning also saw the UFO moving across the sky in an easterly direction, thus confirming Deputy Spaur's report. Among the other observers were

Patrolman H. Wayne Huston of East Palestine, Ohio; Police Chief Gerald Buchert of Mantua, Ohio; and Patrolman Frank Panzanella of Conway, Pennsylvania. Shortly after this historic encounter, both Earl Neff and Donald E. Keyhoe, the director of the then largest civilian saucer group, National Investigations Committee on Aerial Phenomena (NICAP) in Washington, D.C., regretted that so many law enforcement officers and other credible witnesses remain clammed up about their UFO encounters due to the aura of ridicule that had come to surround all aspects of the phenomenon.

Saucerian Press publisher Gray Barker of Clarksburg, West Virginia, made a special trip to attend the 10 November 1973 flying saucer presentation by Cleveland, Ohio, ufologist Earl J. Neff, held in the Soldiers and Sailors Memorial Hall in Pittsburgh, Pennsylvania. Neff investigated hundreds of UFO reports from around the United States and Canada and came to strongly believe in the extraterrestrial hypothesis. He also funded two teenagers in Northeast Ohio, Alan T. Weston of Maple Heights and Raymond A. Keller of Bedford, to publish the famous *Flying Saucer Report*.

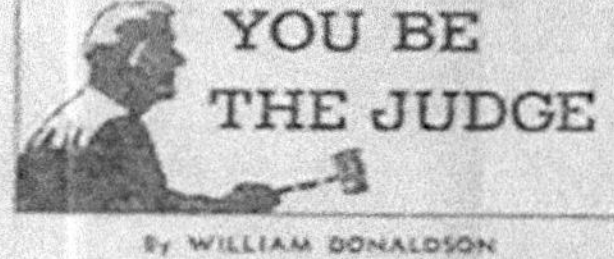

National Enquirer – Volume 44 – No. 15 – Dec 14, 1969

Sighting UFO Sparks Two Teen-Agers Into Publishing Flying Saucer Magazine

By SELIG ADLER

Two Cleveland-area youngsters saw an Unidentified Flying Object as they returned from a Scout trip two years ago, and they've been talking about it ever since.

For it was that first sight of something that looked like a Flying Saucer which inspired Alan Weston and Raymond Keller, who are now both 15, to write, edit and publish a magazine which has now firmly established itself with six issues so far, The Flying Saucer Report.

It looks as if Alan and Raymond have found themselves not only a cause but a profession.

It takes all the time they can spare from schoolwork to put out their magazine, which sells for 25 cents a copy and has a subscription list of over 200, stretching right across the nation.

And their cause is to tell the sober, balanced truth about UFOs — neither scorning all reports as crackpot nonsense, nor believing everything they hear.

It is a rather adult, conservative attitude for two such young men. They didn't arrive at it all at once. Their first issue, in September 1966, was rather wild, and billed itself as "The World's Most Authoritative and Truest Account of Today's Great UFO Invasion!"

Nowadays they are more cautious, but they're still hoping to be convinced, and ready to study the evidence of each report.

They still remember that first glimpse which pointed their lives in this direction. It was on Oct. 7, 1967.

Weston recalled in a recent interview. "The sighting was not dramatic. It was a dark-shaped object, silver in color. It made no sound and it flew at slow speeds about 1,000 feet overhead, for about 20 seconds."

Both boys live in Cleveland suburbs, Weston in Maple Heights and Keller in nearby Bedford.

There is a Cleveland club devoted to UFO information, the Cleveland [Ufology Society, and they reported their sighting to it.]

SAW SAUCER: Raymond Keller holds sketch of silver UFO which he and his pal saw about 1,000 feet overhead, flying slowly and majestically.

OPEN-MINDED PUBLISHERS: Keller (left) and Alan Weston, both 15, hold several issues of their magazine "The Flying Saucer Report," which generates correspondence from all over the world.

YOU BE THE JUDGE

By WILLIAM DONALDSON

AN INTERVIEW WITH EARL J. NEFF

On the morning of 16 October 1971, Cleveland, Ohio's "Dean of Ufology," Earl J. Neff, arrived at the Toronto International Airport, where he was met by Gene

Duplantier, the editor of *Saucers, Space and Science,* Canada's preeminent UFO magazine published in the Toronto suburb of Willowdale, Ontario. Duplantier was to drive Neff to Barrie, Ontario, where he was scheduled to give a lecture on the UFO phenomenon later that evening. Barrie is about an hour's drive due north of Willowdale, so Duplantier took Neff to his Willowdale home so he could rest up first, before proceeding on to Barrie. Neff slept to about 11:30 a.m.; and Duplantier fixed him some lunch. After getting some good food in their stomachs, and since they still had some time to kill before heading up north for the meeting, Duplantier asked Neff, one of North America's outstanding UFO lecturers, if he wouldn't mind being interviewed for a future article in *Saucers, Space and Science.* Neff consented.

Here is the transcript:

Gene: Can you tell me what has become of Major Donald E. Keyhoe since his retirement from the National Investigations Committee on Aerial Phenomena (NICAP)?

Earl: I talked to him just recently on the phone; and his book was scheduled for August. He said he'd like to bring it out in October; but now it probably won't be out until January, because January is a good month for publishers. He is still working on it. The delay is probably due to the fact the publishers had other ideas than Keyhoe's, and probably they were about his stand. He has conformed to their particular wishes.

Gene: Major Keyhoe propounded the extraterrestrial hypothesis as the source of UFOs. Do you think the statement is still valid, considering the technological and scientific advances of today?

Earl: On 6 April, the Cleveland Ufology Project (CUP) had its big banquet at Esterhurst; and in time for that, Major Keyhoe wrote me exactly what he felt about UFOs. He said, "I believe that UFOs are extraterrestrial probes or observation devices controlled by a more advanced civilization carrying out a long survey of our world for some important reason which has not yet been determined."

Gene: Do you feel the same way?

Earl: Yes, definitely.

Gene: There is an upsurge of thought among scientists and investigators that UFOs are a paraphysical-psychic manifestation, rather than from other planets. How do you view this? Are these compatible to your way of thinking?

Earl: No, they are not. In fact, I don't discount that there are coronas and visual sightings that are definitely of a very materialistic nature and that there are others that are mystical and the type that Jung and Freud referred to. But I frankly feel that when you take a 22-calibre rifle, aim at one of these, as has been done on numerous occasions, and you hear it go ping when it hits, you're not hitting an illusion or a mystical thing.

Gene: So probably they could have not just one origin, but two or more.

Earl: Yes, that is quite possible; and I think quite frequently people had a visual experience and others, with all sincerity, had something of a more psychical nature.... I'm not belittling that angle of it; but I do say, like Phillip Klass (a noted aviation authority and skeptic of the time- R.K.), that these are all a corona, etc., etc. type.

Gene: Do you feel that the United Nations (UN), if given the go-ahead, could reasonably solve the UFO mystery?

Earl: Well, if the UN did the same with us that they have done with most of the others, I'm afraid it would be longer than my lifetime.

Gene: According to researchers, UFOs seem to have been here since time immemorial. If this is so, do you personally think the mystery will be solved by the end of the century?

Earl: Well, I'm not a Jeane Dixon (a well-known psychic of the time- R.K.); but I know her well, and think greatly of her. She said to me on a program one night, that by the year 2000, we would take them for granted. We would look at the sky and look at them as we look at aeroplanes today. They would be so numerous we would no longer bother to get excited.

Gene: Accepting the proposition that the mystery is solved, what developments can you see in store for us as inhabitants of Earth? Would the results be beneficial or repugnant to us?

Earl: Frankly, I'm very worried. I don't try to express this thought too generally because if I do, too many people go home and have to take an Exedrin tablet. Major Colman Von Keviczky, whose group appointed me their American representative, when questioned on something of this kind, feels that this is something we should be very much concerned about; and this is the reason we are trying to get Canada, and all of the nations interested and involved in the UN, to consider this very seriously, because we should not have a shoot-down order. We should look at them in a friendly way, which we are not doing at the present time.

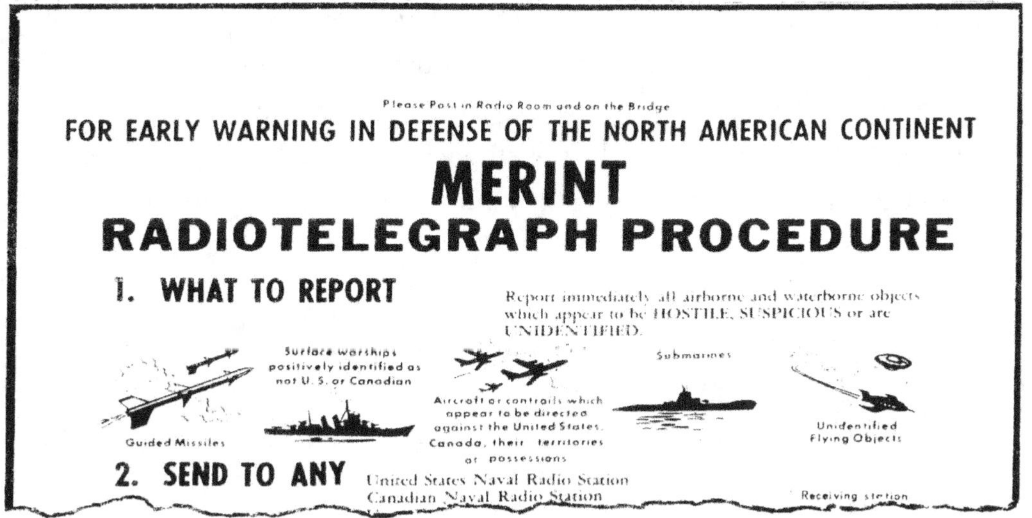

Excerpt of *Merint Report* from files of Cleveland ufologist Earl J. Neff clearly demonstrate that in the early 1970s, the United States Navy considered UFO sightings to be a serious matter and a concern for national security.

The *Merint Report*, which took me from six to eight months to obtain, is the poster that is on all United States naval vessels and tells what to do in case there is a warship, other than ours, within our territory: an aeroplane, a rocket or a submarine other than ours…. or a UFO. We take this very seriously; and yet we have this ridiculous shoot-down order. Even Albert Einstein pleaded with Harry Truman when he was president, not to let our planes shoot at them when 52 monitor-type devices were over Washington, DC. One was hit. Admiral Herbert B. Knowles was with your own Canadian Wilbert Smith in Washington at the time. This piece of metal, this chunk, fell. This is something that has been of great interest to everyone who was involved in it. It was metal unknown to us.

Gene: Were you disappointed that the Apollo astronauts did not find life on the Moon or any evidence of alien visitations?

Earl: I was contacted by a television personality immediately following Apollo 15 and was asked if I'd learned anything further on this flight; and I said "No." He said, "Don't you feel they're highly indoctrinated, the same as the Air Force boys are?" and I said, "Yes, I feel that." In yesterday's news (15 October 1972), a big statement was made for the first time publicly, that in March of last year the Moon had a big geyser erupt. That proves that under the surface of the Moon there is water, something that never before has been known.[6] I wouldn't be surprised that Mr. Kaltenborn was censored off the air- at least that is what we think happened- because he was stopped in the middle of a sentence when he said that he had something very important to say, relative to the flight before the last.

---

[6]   An Associated Press report dated 27 October 2020 from Cape Canaveral, Florida, reported that, "The Moon's shadowed, frigid nooks and crannies may hold frozen water in more places and in larger quantities than previously suspected. And, for the first time, the presence of water on the Moon's sunlit surface has been confirmed, scientists reported Monday (26 October 2020)." This is especially good news for future astronauts inhabiting lunar bases that will be able to tap into these sources of water for drinking and making rocket fuel. Dr. Paul O. Hayne, an astronomer from the University of Colorado at Boulder, writing in the 26 October 2020 issue of *Nature Astronomy* (Springer Nature, Berlin, Germany), noted that while previous observations have indicated that there are millions of tons of ice in the permanently shadowed craters at both the north and south polar regions of the Moon, the new discovery of more than 15,400 square miles of lunar terrain having the capability to trap water in the form of ice, "take the availability of lunar surface water to a new level." This represents an area of ice 20% more expansive than previously estimated by astronomers. See "Moon holds more water than ever thought," Associated Press article in the *Dominion Post* newspaper, 27 October 2020, Morgantown, West Virginia.

Perils of Neo-colonialism Department

Source: ***Dominion Post,*** **Morgantown, West Virginia, 1 November 2020.**

Gene: A proposed future Apollo Moon shot would be to the crater Gassendi. Do you think the so-called "city street layouts" in the crater were made by intelligent beings, or is it mere fantasy on the part of some UFO buffs?

Earl: I'm inclined to think it is fantasy. One night I had George Van Tassel on the air with me from his home at Giant Rock, California. I said, "George, you claim you have a photograph of the city on the Moon. Would you like to tell us about it?" He said, "Yes, I got that photograph." When we asked him to send us a copy of the print, he said, "Now, I really wouldn't know exactly where it is." Well now, if I was asked if I had a piece of UFO metal, I wouldn't say, "Yes, I have piece of UFO metal. It's in my garage; and I've got so much metal out there, I wouldn't know where it is." I think I would prize this very highly. And so, when we checked this thing out, I think it was more imagination than anything else. He did have something and he showed it on his *Proceedings* journal; but when we checked with Mt. Palomar, Palomar was very, very ignorant about it.

Gene: The United States' funding of space exploration has been slowed down considerably. Do you think this will have any effect on our meeting aliens or spacecraft?

Earl: Frank Edwards (prominent radio personality and UFO investigator) said that within the next five years (just before his death – 23 June 1967), we will have contact with an actual spacecraft and person, and that will be by one of our astronauts. Edwards died on the day before the twentieth anniversary of Kenneth Arnold's sighting. I certainly feel that every time we go out there in space, they are highly concerned; and I made public for the first time anywhere in the country that when our experimental shot took place years ago at Cape Kennedy, the object leaving the pad was followed by four UFOs- two above it, one below it, and one behind it. They followed the capsule in that order for one complete orbit of the Earth; and as suddenly as they arrived, they disappeared. This apparently meant that their mission was accomplished. What it was, I don't know. But they are concerned with what we are doing, unquestionably so. One of the slides I have, given to me by Leonard Stringfield, shows an actual UFO- a controversial one- just on the outside edge of the smoke-ball of an experimental hydrogen bomb.

Gene: You were the first to interview Woodrow Derenberger (a contactee from West Virginia) on the air. Can you tell us briefly any latest developments in his contacts with Indrid Cold or others of like nature?

Earl: Monday night, 18 October, on the *Alan Douglas Show*, he will tell all his latest stories. He says he is not crazy. He really had an experience. I had not bought the story hook, line and sinker. I feel that he has elaborated too much. He may have had an original experience; and I am not saying he didn't, because I wasn't there. I have interviewed him at length and have had him on two shows. Fifty percent of his story does check out.

Gene: People are still questioning the whereabouts of George Hunt Williamson (1926-1986; an archaeologist and witness to George Adamski's original encounter with a Venusian in the California desert). Do you know what happened to him?

Earl: I really couldn't say. Someone said that he was in Europe, another said in South America and still another said he was in the country (USA). But I do believe that he is very much alive. (Williamson was a veteran of the Army Air Corps in World War II. In the early 1960s, he legally changed his name to Michel d'Obrenovic and was ordained a priest in the Assyrian Church of the East, sometimes referred to as the Nestorian Church. He died at his home in Santa Barbara, California, on 25 January 1986 and is buried in Arlington National Cemetery in Virginia, memorial identification 99822446. –Cosmic Ray)

Gene: In the book, *Interrupted Journey*, by John G. Fuller, when Betty Hill was under hypnosis, she mentioned a map relating to where her captors came from. Did you find something interesting about that?

Earl: John Fuller may have known the following, but if he did, he left it out of his book. I don't believe he did, because I can't imagine an author as fine as he, not putting this in. When Betty was regressed (put under hypnosis) by Dr. Benjamin Simon, she told how she had seen a map which was relative to the trade routes, the places where the people (the ETs) were going most frequently, and those routes that were seldom used, etc. Now what he didn't say was- what seems of foremost importance to me- was that this map was not a map on a wall. It was not on a piece of paper. It was not on a two-dimensional ground. This was a three-dimensional map. Apparently, it's like when we take a laser beam. Down in Akron, Ohio, just a number of months ago, there was a very beautiful exhibit there. I didn't see it; but it was described to me. It was all about laser beams. You can really think you are seeing something in three dimensions and you can walk right through the blamed thing. This was apparently the type of map she saw.

OBSERVATIONS OF THE "COSMIC RAY"

While Neff was directing the investigations of the Cleveland Ufology Project (CUP), he was also the Ohio state representative for Donald E. Keyhoe's National Investigations Committee on Aerial Phenomena (NICAP), an organization which did not recognize the validity of any direct extraterrestrial contact claims. Neff, when apart from NICAP, was more open to the idea of direct contact. However, he was always cognizant that he needed to temper his enthusiasm and remarks about both George Van Tassel and Woodrow Derenberger when making statements for public record. At the CUP meetings and in the gatherings that followed in a local Parma diner, Neff was more open about the contact incidents and some of his investigations in this area, as well as sharing some of his own personal "metaphysical" experiences. Working with Earl J. Neff on saucer investigations was one of the greatest blessings in my life. Godspeed to you, Earl, wherever you are in this vast and intriguing Cosmos!

NEBRASKA PATROLMAN ENCOUNTERS VENUSIANS IN LANDED SAUCER

Ashland, Nebraska, Police Officer Herbert Schirmer (1945-2017), at age 22, not long after his 3 December 1967 UFO Close Encounter of the Third Kind. Schirmer was a veteran of the United States Navy, serving 1964-1967, before joining the Ashland Police Department. Source: *National Enquirer*

At 2:20 a.m. on the cold and snowy night of 3 December 1967, an Ashland (Saunders County), Nebraska, police officer, Herbert (Herb) Schirmer, then 22 years of age, was on his routine patrol on State Highway 6, just south of the city limits, when two unusually bright red and blinking lights caught his attention, seemingly hovering over the intersection of State Highway 6 (Grand Army of the Republic Highway) and Route 63. about a quarter of a mile further to the southwest of his position. Initially, Schirmer thought the lights belonged to a large, parked truck. But as he sped up to close in on the lights, he soon realized that they were entirely something else, something beyond his wildest imagination.

The red blinking lights were emanating from the portholes of a metallic, semi-spherical UFO, the kind that one might think to be a typical flying saucer. Approaching the object even closer with his cruiser, Schirmer noticed that it had some kind of walkway along its circumference, and that there was an assembly of landing gear dangling beneath it. The officer vaguely recalls the object hovering at a slight tilt some 6 to 8 feet above the highway, touching down momentarily with its landing gear, and then slowly floating upward, all the while making a whining noise like a siren. Schirmer poked his head out of the car's driver-side window and took notice that the flying saucer was again hovering briefly, and then passed slowly overhead, issuing an intense flame and then speeding off in a flash into the distance and out of sight.

With the UFO out of the area, Schirmer felt it was safe to get out of his cruiser and to inspect the highway surface where the object had been hovering just above it and had briefly touched down. Schirmer took his flashlight with him, but upon shining its beam onto the pavement of the landing zone, saw no signs of the flying saucer having ever been there. The officer looked at his wrist watch and noted that he had been out there on the highway almost 30 minutes already. He was baffled, however, as he had a gut feeling that he had only been out on the road for no more than ten minutes, at best. The patrolman then took out his pocket logbook and wrote the following: "Saw a flying saucer at the junction of Highways 6 and 63. Believe it or not!"

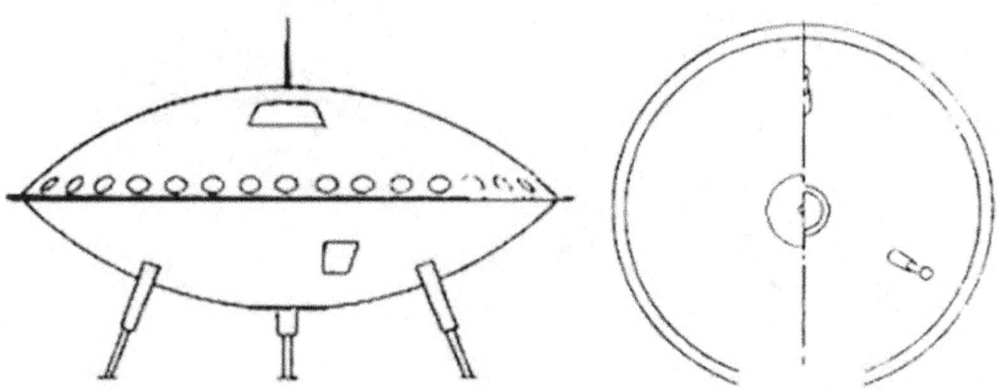

Schematic drawing of flying saucer encountered by Patrolman Herbert Schirmer on 3 December 1967 on the outskirts of Ashland, Nebraska. Source: NICAP Archives

As the patrolman's graveyard shift was over, he immediately returned to the Ashland Police Headquarters to file his report. Once back at the police station, he began to suffer from a headache. Schirmer was hearing an incessant and "weird buzzing" in his head; and discovered that he had somehow acquired a "red welt," approximately two inches long and half an inch wide, on the back of his neck. The welt was located over the "nerve cord" just below his right ear. As it was early Sunday morning and every establishment in Ashland was closed, Police Chief Bill Wlaskin sent Schirmer home and told him to take the next two days off so he could get some needed rest and get checked out by a doctor on Monday morning. He wouldn't have to come back into the office until his regularly scheduled graveyard shift on Tuesday night.

Later at 7:48 a.m. on that Sunday morning of 3 December, with the break of day, Chief Bill Wlaskin, viewing Schirmer as a very competent officer and taking his UFO report seriously, went out to the scene of the alleged encounter to look it over in the emerging daylight, where he happened upon a small, metallic artifact that he could not identify any practical use for. A subsequent chemical analysis of the artifact carried out at the University of Colorado at Boulder by metallurgists contracted with the United States Air Force-sponsored Scientific Study of UFOs, a.k.a. Dr. Edward U. Condon's UFO Committee (1966-1968), revealed its composition to be of iron and silicon. The Boulder scientists speculated that the artifact was most likely "ordinary corroded earthly waste."

Sketch by Wes Crum from NICAP Archives based on Nebraska Patrolman Herbert Schirmer's description of the flying saucer interior.

A little more than two months later, on 13 February 1968, Schirmer was flown into Boulder to undergo hypnosis sessions supervised by Dr. Leo R. Sprinkle of the Department of Psychology at the University of Wyoming at Laramie, who was brought in to the Condon Committee as a psychological consultant on cases of alleged UFO contact and/or abduction. Dr. Sprinkle had also accomplished such hypnosis sessions on UFO experiencers before, on behalf of the then two largest civilian UFO investigations groups in the United States, these being the National Investigations Committee on Aerial Phenomena (NICAP) in Washington, D.C., and the Aerial Phenomena Research Organization (APRO) of Tucson, Arizona. Dr. Sprinkle also wrote the introduction to my first UFO book, Dr. Raymond A. Keller, *Venus Rising: A Concise History of the Second Planet* (Terra Alta, West Virginia: Headline Books, 2015). I was an active member of APRO since 1967 until its closure in 1988, when it was largely superseded by the Mutual UFO Network (MUFON), with its headquarters then in Seguin, Texas.

In the hypnosis sessions conducted by Dr. Sprinkle on the campus of the University of Colorado at Boulder on 14 and 15 February 1968, patrolman Schirmer revealed that, "I tried to radio in (the UFO report); I had one hand on the mike and the other on my gun; but the beam of light that came from the underside of the object kept me from doing anything."

Ashland Police Chief Bill Wlaskin came up to Boulder with Schirmer and was with him during the hypnosis sessions. Wlaskin provided NICAP's Director, Retired Marine Corps Major and aviator Donald E. Keyhoe, with a written report stating that while under hypnosis, Schirmer explained that when a beam flooded his cruiser with light, a small human form, approximately five feet tall, came from beneath the craft and approached him. The Ashland patrolman also said that this small being communicated with him "in some manner" (ESP?) about events that would take place in the United States in the coming years and relayed information about how their ships "operated against gravity."[7]

Schirmer, under a deep trance, allegedly informed Dr. Sprinkle that there were other beings onboard and that they had come from Venus and were in Nebraska for the purpose of siphoning off energy from a nearby nuclear power plant. Additionally, Schirmer detailed the short tour he was given of the spaceship. He was informed that although these beings hailed from Venus, their point of origin was in another solar system and that besides Venus, they also have bases on the back side of the Moon, other planets and their attendant moons in our own solar system, and even on Earth underground and undersea off the coasts of Florida and Argentina.

---

[7] "Hypnotized Policeman Reports Encounter," *U.F.O. Investigator*, Vol. IV, No. 5, (Washington, D.C.: NICAP, March 1968), 1.

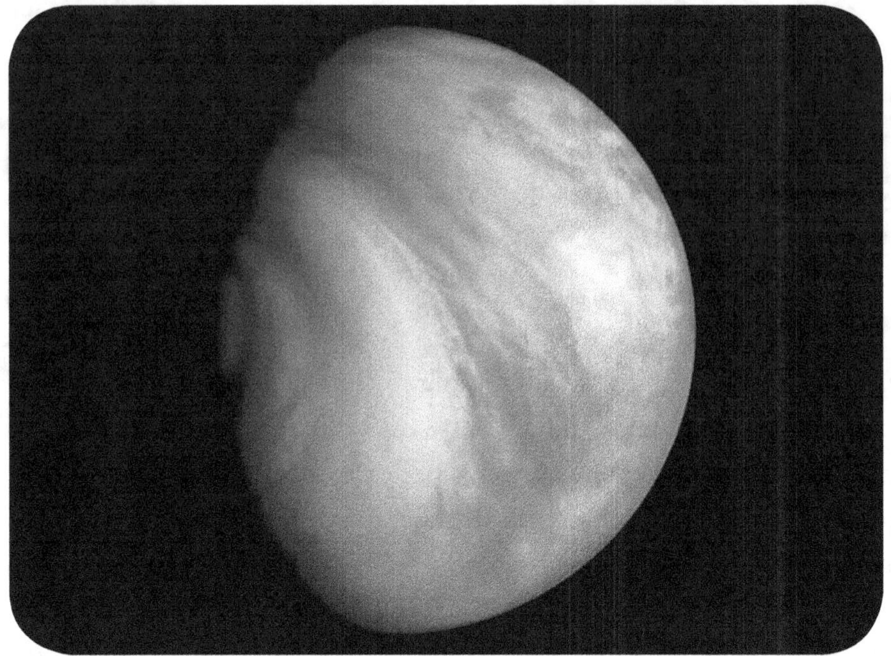

Earth's twin sister planet: Photo taken by Japanese Space Agency's Akatsuki probe in orbit around Venus in 2015.

VINDICATIONS

While the scientists associated with the Condon Committee dismissed Schirmer's claims about aliens coming to Earth from Venus, based on our sister planet allegedly being too hot to support "life as we know it," we need to keep in mind that many of the contactees from the 1950s and the early 1960s, like George Adamski, Albert Coe, Daniel Fry, Annabel Krebbs, Gloria Lee, Howard and Connie Menger, Dr. Frank E. Stranges and George Van Tassel, have affirmed that intelligent beings from the planet Norca in the Tau Ceti system, were the original humanoid inhabitants of Venus, arriving there in space arks some 25 million years ago as their home world was dying, being turned into a vast desert as their planet moved too close to their sun of Tau Ceti due to extreme perturbations in its orbital path. Venus is also the governing planet in the Galactic Confederation, a star alliance consisting of 51 solar systems and 601 planetary members. Therefore, there are many extraterrestrial races living on Venus along with the Norcans, largely underground. The flying dragon (called a "Garuda" on Venus) symbol on the aliens' uniforms may be representative of their planetary ethnic identification within the Confederation. This was all explained by George Van Tassel during the proceedings of the First Interplanetary Spacecraft Convention held at Giant Rock Airport, Landers Field in Southern California, 2-4 April 1954, with the details of this historic assembly provided in my third UFO book, *Cosmic Ray's Excellent Venus Adventure* (Terra Alta, West Virginia: Headline Books, 2017).

Incidentally, despite the cover-up of life on Venus foisted on the American public by the National Aeronautics and Space Administration (NASA) following their Mariner 2 fly-by of Venus in 1962 and measurements of extreme electrical heat in the Venusian ionosphere at three spots on the limb of that planet, it should be noted that the Science Service in Washington, D.C., reported new evidence for life on Venus on 25 April 1964, which was virtually ignored by NASA and blacked out by the American media. There was "direct evidence" presented for water vapor on Venus by Dr. John Strong of Johns Hopkins University in Baltimore, Maryland, who announced that his discovery was made via unmanned balloon flights launched high into Earth's atmosphere. Dr. Strong emphasized that, "It forces us to re-examine every previous calculation concerning the possibility of some kind of life existing on the planet." Dr. Strong charged that, "Too many people have a 'closed mind' concerning the existence of some form of life on Venus." To this astute professor of astronomy, he considered the question of life on Venus still to be "wide open," thus giving credence to the assertions of Herbert Shirmer and all the other contactees that came before and after him.

NEW JERSEY UFO FLAP WITH POSSIBLE UFONAUT SIGHTING

Date: 19 January 1976
Location: Heislerville, New Jersey, USA
Source: Brad Pratt, **"20 Policemen Sighted Enormous UFO,"** *National Enquirer*, Lantana, Florida, 30 March 1976

Mr. and Mrs. Wayne Tomlin of Heislerville, New Jersey, located some 30 miles southwest of Atlantic City, New Jersey, situated on the Delaware Bay, reported seeing "two enormous bright lights, like headlights," only 300 yards away and hovering over a tree line, at about 7:30 p.m. on Monday, 19 January 1976. The lights remained visible for approximately 6 minutes.

Date: 19 January 1976
Location: Dorothy, New Jersey, USA
Source: Brad Pratt, **"20 Policemen Sighted Enormous UFO,"** *National Enquirer*, Lantana, Florida, 30 March 1976

Mrs. Charles Morris of Dorothy, New Jersey, located some 15 miles wet of Atlantic City, New Jersey, reported seeing "a very brilliant red light, the most brilliant red I've ever seen," at about 8 p.m. "I was really overawed by the thing," she noted.

From files of the *National Enquirer,* journalist and police officer describe their UFO encounter along the New Jersey shore.

Date: 20 January 1976
Location: Ventnor, New Jersey, USA
Source: Brad Pratt, **"20 Policemen Sighted Enormous UFO,"** *National Enquirer,* Lantana, Florida, 30 March 1976

On Tuesday, 20 January 1976, at around 5:10 a.m., an enormous, brilliantly glowing UFO shot in from the ocean sky so close to the shoreline of Atlantic City, New Jersey, that a police officer and local reporter, *Atlantic City Free Press* newspaper correspondent Sonny Schwartz on the beach in Ventnor, New Jersey, could not help but see and be awed by its radiance in the morning sky.

Ventnor is an Atlantic City suburb situated on the shoreline; and the officer, then 28 years-old patrolman Frank Ingargiola, and on the Ventnor contingent of the police force since 1971, said that the UFO was so large that, "It could have swallowed me up." The patrolman further noted that upon sighting the object, "I immediately backed my car up a ramp and off the beach." Ingargiola reported that he kept the UFO in sight for some twenty minutes and also affirmed that some twenty other police officers from throughout the Atlantic City area, besides himself and the reporter Schwartz, whom he was driving home that morning, had witnessed it.

"All of a sudden, the object came straight in toward us," said Ingargiola. The patrolman, also a Navy veteran, emphatically declared that, "I've been on a good many midnight watches at sea. I was trained to identify different shapes at night. I've never seen anything like this before. It came in very, very close, just above the breakers, about 500 feet from the car. It was so hughe it seemed to fill the whole windshield. I couldn't see anything else."

Ingargiola also remarked that, "It had a very bright, white light in its center, with a yellowish haze around it twice the size of the light. When it got close, you could see three small, reddish points in it, in the shape of a triangle. Unfortunately, we did not have a camera with us to take a picture of it." The patrolman did note that immediately after the sighting, he had radioed police headquarters in Atlantic City to see if other officers in the area had reported seeing anything unusual in the sky. He was then that Ingargiola was assured by the dispatcher that some twenty other officers had also reported seeing the UFO.

The *Atlantic City Free Press* reporter, then 35 years-old, said of the UFO, "Yes, it was enormous. I could not believe that any light could be so bright. As we looked, we became transfixed by it."

Some of the other Atlantic City police reports of UFOs made during this time included:

Patrolman Daniel Conver was watching the UFO along with his partner, fellow patrolman Daniel Wilhelmy. Said Conver, "The light seemed to get dimmer and then brighter as we watched." Of the UFO encounter, Wilhelmy noted that, "We checked for helicopters; but there weren't any up that night. Patrolman Henry Madanda also witnessed the UFO. Like Ingargiola, he explained that, "It appeared to be a glowing light out over the ocean. As I gazed at it, suddenly it just disappeared in front of my eyes. I was shocked!"

Date: 20 January 1976
Location: Ventnor, New Jersey, USA
Source: Cliff Linedecker, **"Policeman and Reporter Tell 'Scary' Encounter with UFO 'Spaceman,'"** *National Tattler*, Chicago, Illinois, 11 April 1976.

Additional information came to light concerning Ventnor, New Jersey, patrolman Frank Ingargiola and *Atlantic City Free Press* (New Jersey) correspondent Sonny Schwartz' UFO encounter, which was published in the 11 April 1976 issue of the

Chicago, Illinois-based tabloid, *National Tattler*. Apparently, this UFO sighting also involves the report by these two of a UFO occupant walking on the beach. According to *National Tattler* reporter Cliff Linedecker's account of the UFO incident, "Ingargiola sent out an urgent call for help on his police radio. Seven squad cars containing 16 policemen arrived at the beach within minutes. They saw a bright light moving out into the Atlantic Ocean before it finally disappeared on the horizon."

This report is in sharp contrast to the article that appeared in the *National Enquirer* just 12 days earlier. In that article, patrolman Ingargiola simply conducted a radio check to determine if any other officers had seen and reported the UFO, of which some twenty of his associates apparently had, radioing in their observations to police headquarters in Atlantic City. In this report, however, some 16 police officers actually rendezvous with Ingargiola and the reporter Schwartz on the Ventnor beach, not far from the famous Atlantic City Boardwalk.

In the more sensational article, Linedecker further writes that, "Both Ingargiola and Schwartz believe there was some connection between the UFO and a strange, seven-foot creature they saw lurking along the Boardwalk." He claims to have interviewed Ingargiola about this creature sighting, in which the patrolman explained, "I'll admit I was scared. When that thing (UFO) turned toward us, it was no more than 30 feet off and the ground about 100 feet away."

Reporter Schwartz allegedly confirmed Ingargiola's observational remarks, and stated, "I'm taking UFO reports a lot more seriously now." He also added that he was puzzled by a weird-looking individual at least six and one-half feet tall with immense broad shoulders they saw just after spotting the UFO. "There was something absolutely inhuman about the sight of him (the alleged UFO occupant) walking down the Boardwalk."

Both the *Enquirer* and *Tattler* agree that this entire episode began sometime around 5:10-5:15 a.m., just after Ingargiola offered journalist Schwartz a ride. The *Enquirer* declared that Ingargiola was going to give Schwartz a ride home, while the *Tattler* article reported that Ingargiola was going to give Schwartz a lift back to his newspaper office. In any event, they were still in Ventnor and driving slowly when they first noticed a spherical light surrounded in a green-yellow haze moving parallel to their course along the beach.

GEORGE LESNICK: CONNECTICUT'S "UFO COP"

Fairfield, Connecticut, Police Lieutenant George Lesnick (1929-2010), the "UFO Cop," brought a scientific investigative approach to ufology in addition to a high degree of credibility. Photo source: Obituary, *Review-Journal* (Las Vegas, Nevada)

At a few minutes before midnight on Wednesday, 24 March 1976, Fairfield, Connecticut, Police Sergeant George Lesnick received a call at department headquarters from off-duty Officer Frank Nolfi reporting "something strange" that he was then observing in the sky above Eleven O'Clock Road in the Greenfield Hills suburb of the city. Nolfi's shift had ended at 11:00 p.m. and he was driving home. What he witnessed hovering over Eleven O'Clock Road were six luminous, sphere-shaped objects. Sergeant Lesnick and Detective Ronald Thompson got into a patrol car and drove out to Eleven O'Clock Road to see these UFOs for themselves. Arriving on the scene, Lesnick and Thompson got out of their vehicle to get an unobstructed view of the UFOs. Lesnick had no idea what they were and later told James Lomuscio, a staff writer for the Westport, Connecticut *Fairpress,* that, "It was six objects. One was larger than the other five and roundish. They were like very white, bright lights; and the largest one was bright orange." By the time that Lesnick and Thompson espied the UFOs, Lesnick noted that, "They were moving at an incredible rate of speed and then stopping in the sky where one would go east, one would go west, and stop abruptly."[8]

As it turned out, Officer Nolfi, Sergeant Lesnick, and Detective Thompson weren't the only witnesses to the UFO activity that night. There were also two Easton, Connecticut, police officers and hundreds of other civilian observers from as far away as Hartford, Connecticut's capital city. In summing up the UFO episode, Lesnick noted, "We checked the airports and there were no aircrafts in the area. It was a clear night, nothing I could explain, and hundreds of people spotted the same thing."

Sergeant Lesnick, on the date of the UFOs sighting, was 57-years-old and had been serving on the Fairfield police force since 1956. His close encounter with the UFOs marked the beginning of an unsatiable interest in the UFO phenomenon. He literally immersed himself in UFO books and literature, seeking an explanation for what he and the other two police officers had witnessed that night. In his pursuit of more UFO information, Lesnick even went so far as to join Dr. J. Allen Hynek's Center for UFO Studies (CUFOS), headquartered in Evanston, Illinois, to the north of Chicago. Dr. Hynek was an astronomer from Northwestern University, also situated in Evanston, Illinois, and formerly the Air Force Technical Consultant on UFOs for over 22 years. CUFOS was always looking for individuals like Lesnick to serve as investigators for the many UFO reports that came to their attention. The investigative experience he gained through extensive years of police work made him perfect for such an assignment in the CUFOS organization.

---

[8]   James Lomuscio, "UFO Cop: A Fairfield policeman finds that seeing is believing," *Fairpress,* Westport, Connecticut, 17 July 1985.

TEAM-UP

By March 1983, George Lesnick had been promoted to the rank of Lieutenant. Of course, in keeping a prudential attitude toward his work in law enforcement, Lesnick would investigate UFO cases only during his off-duty hours. During this time, there was a tremendous flap of UFO activity across the state line in Westchester County, New York. Apparently, a large, boomerang-shaped UFO had made its appearance over Westchester County, and CUFOS had dispatched both Lesnick and Philip Bragano, a Fairfield, Connecticut, resident and astronomer, as well as the Chair of the Science Department at the Windward School in White Plains, New York. Yes, there were other qualified investigators in New York State, but none as geographically close to Westchester County as Lesnick and Bragano, just across the state line and able to reach the area of the UFO flap in a relatively quick drive. Right away, Lesnick received a good impression of Bragano and his scientific credentials. "I knew from the start that we were a good time," declared Lesnick.

Philip Bragano was equally appreciative of George Lesnick, telling the *Fairpress* newspaper correspondent, "I basically did all the technical research and technical evaluation, and he (Lesnick) did all the police work, got all the facts out." In the interviews of UFO witnesses conducted by Bragano and Lesnick, this "Dynamic Duo" of CUFOS ufologists estimated that about 90 percent of the UFOs could ultimately be reclassified as "identified," falling into such mundane categories as weather balloons, conventional aircraft or shooting stars viewed under unusual atmospheric conditions, such as cloud inversions. The remaining 10 percent required follow up with more detailed investigations, perhaps carried out by specialists brought in from CUFOS. The Westchester sightings appeared to fall in this 10 percent category. According to Bragano, many officials from local, state and federal levels of government tried to attribute these sightings to planes flying in a close formation. "But despite four years of sightings," Bragano emphasized, "nobody has ever been able to track down any planes or any pilots, or any airports they are coming from."

George Lesnick affirmed that none of the witnesses to the Westchester boomerang UFO sightings detected any kinds of sound throughout the duration of their encounters, no sounds from any engines. Lesnick explained that this Westchester UFO really stood out among all the many other UFO sightings due to its tremendous size. It was allegedly larger than a football field and only hovering about 500 feet above the ground. "It was so close and so intense a sight," declared Lesnick, "that people stopped their cars on New York's Taconic Parkway and caused accidents."

And on the following day, when George Lesnick drove in to visit the Yorktown Heights, New York, police station to check up on any further UFO reports that had come in during the night, he discovered that its switchboard was still lit up like a Christmas tree with people all throughout the area reporting their sighting of the massive UFO. With respect to the UFO witnesses, of which Lesnick claimed to have interviewed thousands in the past few years, he said, "There were doctors, lawyers, and computer experts. You're talking about credible people seeing incredible things."

UFO Flap Spilled Over into Adjacent Counties

The CUFOS investigators were not at all surprised to discover that this UFO flap had spread beyond Westchester County, New York, spilling over into the neighboring New York counties of Dutchess and Putnam, as well as Fairfield County to the east in Connecticut. Of this aerial commotion, George Lesnick's astronomer associate Philip Bragano opined, "If that was all just attributed to stunt pilots, they would have to have been all over the place, have an unlimited supply of gasoline, and the way they were flying, they would have to be better than the Air Force Blue Angels."

Same UFO Reappears

George Lesnick and Philip Bragano may have thought the UFO sightings of March 1983 were just a fluke, but the men knew they weren't all that rare when what seemed to be the same type of UFOs came back in full force on the momentous night of 24 July 1984. Sightings of the UFOs extended from Danbury, Connecticut to Rockland County, New York. Of at least one of these UFOs, Bragano noted that a columnist for a popular science magazine that the UFO, having a boomerang-shaped appearance, might have been six Cessna airplanes flying in a close formation. "But the wind velocity gusted up to 32 miles per hour that night," said Bragano, the scientific UFO investigator, adding, "And these things were unaffected. Additionally, he continued, "And planes can't hover. It's been hovering for as long as ten minutes." In March of 1985, Bragano declared that he had witnessed similar lights in a V-formation over Fairfield, Connecticut, but officials from the Federal Aviation Administration (FAA) told him that these lights were just planes. "I'm not buying it!" exclaimed the scientifically-meticulous Bragano.

MEMORIES OF THE "COSMIC EGG"

When it comes to UFO sightings, Philip Bragano's memory goes back to the famous appearance of the "Cosmic Egg" in the skies over Newtown, Connecticut, in September 1978. At that time, residents and local officials, to include the police, kept spotting an egg-shaped UFO passing above them at a high altitude. The anomalous object emitted a bright yellow glow, like the Sun, and kept dipping in figure-8 maneuvers. An agent for the Internal Revenue Service, out on an auditing assignment, snapped a photograph of the so-called "Cosmic Egg," which was turned over to CUFOS for computer analysis at their headquarters in Illinois. The conclusions reached in the photo's scrutiny revealed that it was a disc-shaped object some 30-feet in diameter. And the printout showed its contour to match that of a classic flying saucer. Naturally, a spokesperson for the FAA tried to put a damper on the whole episode, calling it a "hoax." Bragano, however, summed it up thusly: "It was really weird."

CLOSE ENCOUNTER OF THE SECOND KIND

Another case which piqued the interest of astronomer Philip Bragano took place in 1979 and involved a Huntington, Connecticut, woman who came into proximity to a 20-feet in diameter, red-glowing sphere in the woods behind her home. As she opened her back door and approached the UFO, it backed away quickly and then seemed to just keep shrinking in size until it couldn't be seen anymore, just drifting away like the bubble the good witch Glinda used to get around with in the land of Oz. "The next day (after her UFO encounter)," noted Bragano, "she woke up and her eyes were red, and her face was red, and her skin was all itchy. She showed the symptoms of being exposed to microwaves. Her doctor diagnosed her condition as 'conjunctivitis, cause unknown.'"

For ufologists like Philip Bragano and his CUFOS associate, George Lesnick, a UFO incident such as this would be considered as a "close encounter of the second kind," because the skin burns from the object would serve as trace evidence of a UFO's presence.

CLOSE ENCOUNTERS OF THE THIRD KIND

As in the title of the 1977 Steven Spielberg movie classic, *Close Encounters of the Third Kind* (Columbia Pictures, Culver City, California), contact with the extraterrestrial pilots of the UFO occur. Retired Police Lieutenant George Lesnick, speaking as an experienced investigator of the UFO phenomenon, readily admits there is a high probability that in some UFO cases, extraterrestrials are arriving on Earth in interplanetary spaceships. "After all," opines Lesnick, "it would be too egotistical to think that the Earth, a tiny piece of driftwood in the universe, is the only planet with life on it."

His partner in ufology, Philip Bragano, heartily concurs with George Lesnick's assessment of the extraterrestrial hypothesis (ETH). Both ufologists agree that one of the more spectacular close encounters of the third kind in the history of New England was the case of Betty Ann (Andreasson) Luca (1937-2022) of Cheshire, Connecticut, who under hypnosis revealed that she was physically abducted aboard an alien craft on the night of 25 January 1967 and medically examined by small, odd-looking, gray-colored beings with large heads, small slits for their noses and all-black eyes. Her unusual experiences with these extraterrestrials are documented in the *New York Times* bestseller-listed book by former Mutual UFO Network (MUFON) Massachusetts State Director Raymond E. Fowler, *The Andreasson Affair* (Englewood Cliffs, New Jersey: Prentice-Hall, Inc., 1979).

The United States government never got out of the UFO investigations business. Northwestern University astronomer, Dr. J. Allen Hynek, Air Force UFO consultant for over 22 years, wrote guidelines in 1975 for FBI agents and law enforcement officials outlining the proper procedures for investigating UFO reports. Project Bluebook was allegedly shut down by the Air Force in 1969. Photo source: *Popular Mechanics* magazine (NYC, NY).

GOVERNMENT UFO COVER-UP CONSIDERED

Fairpress reporter James Lomuscio wondered if any of these so-called "close encounters of the third kind" might have been orchestrated by agents of some TOP SECRET United States government project. Philip Bragano thought it somewhat possible, especially since government agencies were stressing that they were no longer involved in the UFO phenomenon in any way, despite many contraindications coming to light, such as an article by Northwestern University (Evanston, Illinois) astronomy professor and former Air Force UFO consultant for over 22 years, Dr. J.

Allen Hynek's publication of an article in the official Federal Bureau of Investigation (FBI) *Law Enforcement Bulletin* of February 1975 (Washington, D.C., Vol. 44, No. 2), titled "The UFO Mystery," pages 16-20, which clearly outlines the procedures that should be taken by FBI agents and other law enforcement officials when following up and investigating UFO incidents.

By 1985, Police Detective Ronald Thompson, who was with George Lesnick in the patrol car during his original 1976 UFO encounter, affirmed that while he wasn't sure if any of the UFOs were extraterrestrial, he was still sure that what he and Lesnick saw up in the sky that momentous night could not be easily accounted for. "What I really remembered about it was that they (the UFOs) seemed very close. They would be still, and then they would just flash across, like a shooting star. But they didn't look anything like shooting stars, and you are talking to a guy who doesn't believe that UFOs are spaceships from another planet."

WELL-REMEMBERED SOLID CITIZEN

George Andrew Lesnick, a retired Lieutenant for the Fairfield Police Department, beloved husband of Elfriede Barrett Lesnick, of Henderson, Nevada, and formerly of Fairfield, Conn., passed away 31 January 2010 at the age of 81. The son of the late Andrew and Barbara Novak Lesnick, George grew up in Fairfield, graduating from Roger Ludlow High School in 1947, and served in the United States Army, 82nd Airborne Division, during the Korean War. George became a Fairfield police officer in 1956. He was proud of his 29-year career on the police force, and was recognized for numerous accomplishments, retiring as a lieutenant. He moved to Henderson in 1992, where he worked as a security officer for actress Debbie Reynolds and joined the Screen Actors Guild of America, appearing in several movies, television shows and commercials. He was a member of the Fairfield Police Benevolent Association, American Legion, Knights of Columbus and the Law Enforcement Association of Nevada.

WHEN UFOs WERE FIRST DEEMED "ESSENTIALLY REAL" WITH POLICE INVOLVEMENT IN TWO OF FOUR CASES NOTED

Dr. Berthold Eric Schwarz (1924-2010), prominent New Jersey psychiatrist who, starting in 1968, wrote articles in academic medical journals attesting to the credibility of UFO experiencers and the phenomena encountered by them. Photo source: https://www.findagrave.com/memorial/58877556/berthold-e_-schwarz

Abstract: The following article provides a synopsis of Dr. Berthold Eric Schwarz' groundbreaking article on the reality of UFOs that appeared in a prominent Pennsylvania academic medical journal back in 1968, thereby rallying many in the global scientific community to seriously consider the phenomenon and the implications inherent in UFOs as physical and possibly extraterrestrial spacecraft. -Dr. Raymond A. Keller

Scientific Credibility

In October 1968, just one year before the infamous federal government-sponsored University of Colorado at Boulder's infamous *Scientific Study of UFOs* was officially released, directed by that institution's physics chair, Dr. Eduard U. Condon, and totally debunking the entire UFO phenomenon, a handful of scientists from throughout the United States had decided to join the conversation as to the reality of these mysterious objects and the as yet undetermined intelligence behind their evermore frequent appearances in our skies and their occupants, the so-called "ufonauts" alleged interactions with American citizens from all walks of life. Among these were Dr. J. Allen Hynek, an astronomer from Chicago's Northwestern University and Air Force Project Bluebook consultant on UFOs, Dr. Jacques Valle, a French computer expert and long-time investigator of the phenomenon and author of several books on UFOs, as well as Dr. Ronald Leo Sprinkle, a prominent psychologist from the University of Wyoming at Laramie who also served as the first scientific consultant to the Aerial Phenomena Research Organization (APRO), the second largest civilian UFO investigating group in the world, then located in Tucson, Arizona.

Dr. Sprinkle, it should be noted, wrote the introduction to my first book in the *Venus Rising* series. In October 1968, I was a member of APRO, which unfortunately ceased operations in 1988. Much of the group's UFO investigating activities were assumed by the rival Mutual UFO Network (MUFON), then headquartered in Seguin, Texas.

The block of ice encasing the UFO phenomenon began to break even more in October 1968 when Dr. Berthold Eric Schwarz, an assistant attending psychiatrist at Montclair Community Hospital in Montclair, New Jersey, joined the fray in publicly coming out in a prominent academic journal attesting to his conclusion that UFOs were "essentially real," and not delusions or figments of anyone's overactive imagination. In that month's issue of the prestigious medical journal, *Medical Times* (Stroudsburg, Pennsylvania: Romaine Pierson Publications, Vol. 96, No. 10), Dr. Schwarz' article, "UFOs: Delusion or Dilemma," October 1968, focused on four close-range UFO encounters which he personally investigated.[9] Speaking to the UFO witnesses in person, the psychiatrist became convinced that there were no psychopathological reasons for these people to have had these experiences. He concluded that the UFOs involved in each of the four cases were "essentially real;" and hence the UFO phenomenon, in general, was a worthy subject for scientific inquiry.

Police officers were involved in Case One as experiencers, and in Case Four as investigators, which follow:

Competition with Santa's Sleigh

On Christmas Eve of 1966, a factory worker from Passaic County, New Jersey, Claude Coutant, photographed this UFO hovering over the Wanaque Reservoir, the site of intensive UFO activity for several months. The mayor, city councilmen, police officers, security guards and many other credible witnesses reported a UFO emitting a blinding beam of nearly opaque light that would, when the reservoir was frozen over, melt circles in the ice. The UFO flap provoked a military presence in the area, where attempts were made to confiscate all photos of the Wanaque object and to pressure the UFO witnesses into silence. Fortunately, this photo escaped confiscation and many of the UFO experiencers spoke up about their encounters, believing strongly, like police sergeant Benjamin Thompson, whose account appears below, that the truth needed to be known.

---

[9]   The UFO cases were not presented in chronological order in the medical journal by Dr. Schwarz. The order of their presentation is maintained here, with the first two in New Jersey and the second two in Pennsylvania. The New Jersey cases were presented here due to their close proximity to the east central border of Pennsylvania during the period of an extensive UFO flap taking place there.

Case Number One: Wanaque, New Jersey, 11 October 1966
Classification: CE-2
"Blinded by the Light"

Dr. Schwarz read numerous newspaper accounts about a flurry of UFO sightings taking place in the vicinity of Wanaque Reservoir in northwest New Jersey in late September 1966 through January 1967, and then decided to drive out to the area where he first spoke with Sergeant Benjamin Thompson of the Borough of Ringwood Police Department in Passaic County, New Jersey, where the reservoir is located. The police sergeant, respecting Dr. Schwarz' medical and scientific background, was not as reluctant to discuss his UFO encounter as he was with reporters from sundry media, who tended to be more sensationalist in their approach to both him and the subject of UFOs. In his own words, as spoken into Dr. Schwarz' portable tape recorder, Sergeant Thompson describes his UFO encounter that took place on 11 October 1966, starting about 9:15 p.m.:

"It was diagonally 250 feet from me, out over the reservoir, as big as an automobile, or bigger. It was about 250 feet up in the air. When I got out of the police car, this thing was so bright that it blinded me so bad I couldn't find the car. It was all white, like looking into a bulb and trying to see the socket, which you can't do. I signed out of service (to the Borough of Ringwood Police) for twenty minutes because I couldn't see, neither the fingers of my hand nor the lights of my jeep. I stood by the fence until my vision came back gradually.

"It made no sounds, but left a heavy mist-like sort of fog. It really shook me up. When I got back into the car, switched on the red dome light and flasher, and then got out of the car and started walking toward it, it took off. It never made a sound. I would say that I observed it for about three minutes. I was totally blinded, after the light. It took away my voice and I was hoarse for two weeks after that."

Nine months later, Dr. Schwarz interviewed Sergeant Thompson again, and his story did not vary even one iota in the details. The psychiatrist was convinced that Sergeant Thompson's UFO experience was real because several other officers in the Ringwood Police Department confirmed his account and testified to Thompson's outstanding reputation as to never telling a lie or making up tall tales.

Case Number Two: Newfoundland, New Jersey, 15 October 1966
Classification: CE-2
"Flu-like illness induced by UFO encounter"

Here is another UFO encounter that took place in the vicinity of a reservoir in New Jersey. In this case, our UFO experiencer, Jerry H. Simmons was a 22-year-old gentleman from Montclair, New Jersey, a bedroom community of New York City, who was employed as a forester in Newfoundland, New Jersey, a small, unincorporated community in Passaic County, extending more to the eastern end of the county limits and situated in the north central section of the Garden State. Simmons maintained that on Saturday, 15 October 1966, while driving to a campsite that he frequented in the nearby Split Rock Reservoir, between the hours of 4:30 a.m. and 5:00 a.m., his car was buzzed by an anomalous object.

Simmons informed Dr. Schwarz about the incident: "I was traveling north on the road into the campsite and noticed a very outstanding glow in the rearview mirror. I thought at first that my brake light was stuck because it (the UFO) was a very dull glow at the time I noticed it. I tried putting my foot under the brake pedal and pulling it up. It was at this point that I became aware of the orange-red glow becoming brighter."

The forester then parked his car along the side of the road and lowered the window on the driver's side so he could get a better look at the back end of his car. Then, from out of nowhere, came a "huge, glowing light" that seemed to be emerging from some type of "solid body or object" apparently approaching him. At this point of the encounter, Simmons noted that he began to "doubt my sanity," adding that, "I could not accept what my eyes were seeing; but it only took a few seconds for all doubt to leave my mind and for me to understand that what I was seeing was very real."

Deciding to get back into his car and drive south back to the main road, Simmons was hoping that he could flag down assistance or even garner others who might come with him back to the campsite who could serve as witnesses to the UFO(s). He thought that perhaps the light might be a probe of some kind dispatched from the larger, but darker object. Unfortunately for him, the intelligence behind the UFO had other plans. As the object continued to slowly approach him, his car motor died out, thus leaving him stranded on a lonely country backroad.

"Without any warning," asserted the forester, "all the electrical equipment quit working. My headlights, dash lights and engine quit. I don't believe I have ever been so frustrated in all my life."

Once the UFO was directly over his car, it passed over to the passenger side of the vehicle, thus allowing Simmons to turn the ignition and move the vehicle slightly forward down the road. This cat-and-mouse game between the UFO and Simmons occurred two more times, until the UFO intelligence seemingly tired of it and flew out over the reservoir once Simmons had gotten closer to it.

On 17 January 1967, Simmons was admitted to the Montclair Community Hospital for an illness that one of the doctors on staff diagnosed as the "flu." The forester reported that symptoms of "fatigue, anorexia, generalized soreness and weakness of the muscles, drowsiness, chills and a weight loss of 35 pounds" had all plagued him since his initial encounter with the UFO. Doctors and medical staff were concerned about the persistence and severity of these symptoms contributing to the "bizarre nature of the illness." Therefore, arrangements were made for Simmons' admission to the National Institute of Health (NIH) for a special analysis and study, free of charge. The forester, however, did not like the track where this was heading, and declined to participate any further or go to the NIH headquarters in Bethesda, Maryland, across from Johns Hopkins Hospital. Fortunately for the UFO experiencer, all of these aforementioned symptoms disappeared on their own after a few months.

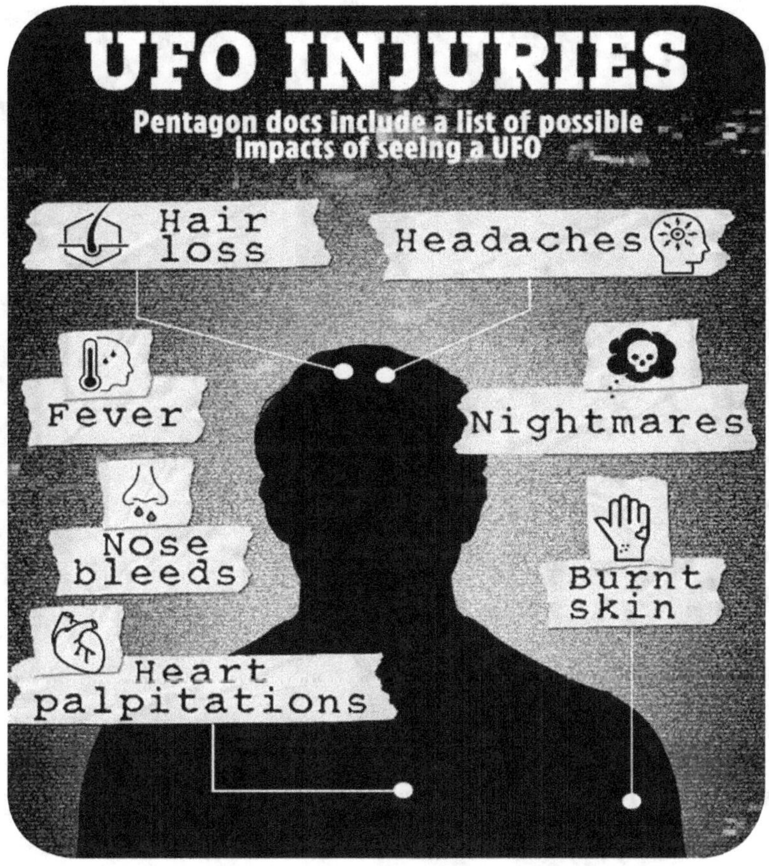

Pentagon doctors warn that not all UFO encounters are happy ones. Artwork source: *The Sun,* U.S., subsidiary of *The Sun*, London, U.K.

MENTAL HEALTH SURVEY CHECKS OUT

In the *Medical Times* article, Dr. Schwarz reported: "A study of the forester's past life, gleaned in several interviews lasting many hours, led me to believe that he never had any previous experiences like this. He had never had any emotional illness. He was an experienced outdoorsman who had camped in many of the states of the United States for some years. He was a high school graduate and had had two additional years of industrial arts."

Perhaps Robert Martz' encounter with UFOs on a rural Pennsylvania road in 1966 inspired this scene with Richard Dreyfuss in Steven Spielberg's epic, *Close Encounters of the Third Kind* (Columbia Pictures, Hollywood, California, 1977).

Case Number Three: Outskirts of Monroeton, Bradford County, Pennsylvania, 25 April 1966
Classification: CE-2
"Stalled pickup truck engine and faded headlights"

While in the process of driving home with a friend, shortly after 8 p.m. on 25 April 1966, Robert W. Martz, a 73-year-old retired electrical contractor, sighted a "fireball-type UFO" in the vicinity of Monroeton, Pennsylvania. According to Martz' testimony, as given to Dr. Schwarz, he and his friend's attention "was drawn to the sky by a very awesome, huge, flaming body, which lit up a large area, and was visible for several seconds. It had a lengthy green and yellow tail."

Soon after the appearance of the first UFO, a second object, cigar-shaped, came into view. Of this UFO, Martz noted that, "A dim light could actually be seen coming from four ports on the craft. It looked like it was 250 feet in front of us and 250 feet up; and it could go at a terrific speed. It was about 25 feet in length and had a tail 35 feet long." The retired contractor added that, "My pickup truck's engine stalled and the headlights faded out. I was amazed and flabbergasted."

Solid Psychological Profile

Dr. Schwarz believed Martz because of his solid psychiatric profile. The psychiatrist duly remarked: "Martz has never had any emotional illness. He and his friends do not use liquor or unprescribed drugs. There was nothing in the contractor's history or behavior since the UFO event to suggest sociopathic behavior, brain syndrome and the like."

Case Number Four: Presque Isle Beach on outskirts of Erie, Erie County, Pennsylvania, 31 July 1966

Classification: CE-3

"Possible contact and monster sighting"

This CE-3 case involved multiple experiencers whose car was stuck in the sand on the Presque Isle beach, immediately to the northwest of Erie, in the northwest corner of Pennsylvania, on the last day of July in 1966. It was around 10 p.m. when Erie Police Patrolman Robert Loeb, Jr., and fellow Patrolman Ralph E. Clark were making their nightly beach patrol in the Presque Isle Peninsula Park when they noticed an automobile bogged down in the sand and stopped to check it out.[10] The occupants of the car were Douglas Tibbets, 18, Betty Jean Klem, 16, Anita Haifley, 22, and Gerald La Belle, 26, the owner of the car, whom the others informed the police had walked into town to try and get some help in removing the automobile from the sand, but who had not yet returned. Upon hearing about La Belle's going for assistance, Senior Patrolman Loeb told the others in the car that, "We'll be back in another 30 or 40 minutes and we will check again if you are still here."

Right after the policemen left, the two young women in the car rolled down the windows to look at the starry night sky when they spotted a bright pinpoint of light that continually seemed to increase in size and luminosity as it was swooping down and nearing their vehicle. Much to their dismay, the illumined, strange object from the heavens landed directly in front of their car, right behind a line of brushy

---

[10] Gabriel Green, *Let's Face the Facts About Flying Saucers* (New York City, New York: Popular Library, 1967), 119-121.

trees. Betty Jean Klem later remarked to representatives of local media, concerning the UFO, "It was the size of a house. It was mushroom-shaped. I could even see lights on the back of it. The thing settled down on the beach about 100 yards from us. When it struck the ground, it then glowed bright red." And Douglas Tibbets, in speaking to the same Erie reporter, added that, "We felt the car shake and then there was a loud noise such as a telephone receiver makes."

A few seconds after the landing of the UFO, all of the car's occupants agreed that the glowing red light gave way to flashing rays of white light that seemed to be probing the beach and woods. Tibbets, in his police report of the incident, noted that, "There were about a dozen lights and they seemed to be searching for some-thing." At the same time as the UFO began to probe the area, all of those inside the car heard scratching noises on the roof of their vehicle. Around 10:30 p.m., the patrolmen returned to the scene of the bogged down vehicle, with their red lights flashing so that those in the car would know it was them on the return patrol. After the patrolmen were back on the scene, Tibbets felt it was safe to get out of the vehicle, whence he found several scratches and a dent in the roof of the car. A conversation then ensued.

Tibbets to the patrolmen: "There are some mighty weird things happening up the beach." The patrolmen then walked with Tibbets to the area in front of the car. Betty Jean Klem, occupying the front passenger seat, leaned over and pressed the automobile's horn, thereby emitting a shattering blare into the dark night.

Patrolman Loeb noted that, "Miss Klem was hysterical, shaking and crying. She sobbed that a giant figure had approached the car." This prompted Tibbets and the patrolmen to hurry back to the car.

Klem: "There's something out there in the dark!" This is what she screamed upon seeing a dark creature approaching the front of the car. She further remarked that, "It did not appear human and it wasn't like any animal I've ever seen. It was over six feet tall and I could not see any arms or legs.[11] When I blew the horn, it slowly

---

[11] Marcus Lowth (ufologist and paranormal investigator), "The Shadow People- Aliens? Ghosts? Or Entities from Another Dimension?" *UFO Insight*, 11 March 2019, https:// www.ufoinsight.com/cryptozoology/bizarre-entities/shadow-people (Accessed 6 September 2019): "While they (the Shadow People) have been seen for centuries, at least according to legends and folklore, it would appear that sightings and general awareness of Shadow People are increasing as we surge forward into the twenty-first century. And while these mysterious, black silhouette-type entities are seemingly at

moved away and disappeared into the bushes." Betty Jean Klem was of the opinion that the darkness of the night kept her from viewing other features of the creature.

Klem leaped from the vehicle once Tibbets and the patrolmen arrived back at the vehicle. Patrolman Clark reported that this is when, "She started to run away and I caught her," thus preventing Klem from hurting herself, possibly tripping over a rotting log or some other artifact on the beach.

Anita Haifley, being in the back seat of the vehicle and huddling over her two small children, did not see anything, but could hear the scratching on the roof. For the sake of her children, she did manage to maintain her composure throughout the incident.

PARK POLICE CHIEF OPINES

Dan Dascanio, Park Police Chief, weighed in on this most unusual incident. "I know what people are going to say;" Dascanio remarked, adding, "but this girl (Klem) definitely saw something that frightened her badly. This is no joke, as far as we (of the Presque Isle Park) are concerned. The girl was a credible person. Of the two individuals involved, she was the most specific about what she saw. She made no attempt to fill in her story when she wasn't sure. She was one scared girl when I first saw her. Her hands were shaking. Her face was trembling. Her speech was more inarticulate; and she had difficulty maintaining her composure. Her eyes were red and she kept shaking her head from side to side." At Dascanio's recommendation, on the following morning at 7:00 a.m. (1 August 1966) after the alleged UFO/alien encounter, two park patrolmen, Paul Wilson and J. Robert Canfield, were dispatched to the site of the incident, which was taped off the night before by Erie patrolmen Loeb and Clark. Later that day, the site was also visited by Erie Patrolman Abert Gagnon, who also checked out the area for anything that Wilson and Canfield may have overlooked. Wilson and Canfield, immediately upon their arrival, noticed distinct impressions in the sand filled with a sticky, but colorless

---

home in the paranormal world of ghosts and apparitions, reports of such beings crop up regularly in case of alien abduction." With so many others in the car and at the scene, as well as the seeming presence of just one entity, it may have prudent in this instance, on the part of the creature, to not follow through with an abduction attempt.

liquid. Samples were taken of this liquid, mixed with sand, and later delivered to the Erie Police Department lab for analysis. Nothing further has been revealed concerning the lab's findings about the liquid, other than that it was mixed with silicon from the sand.

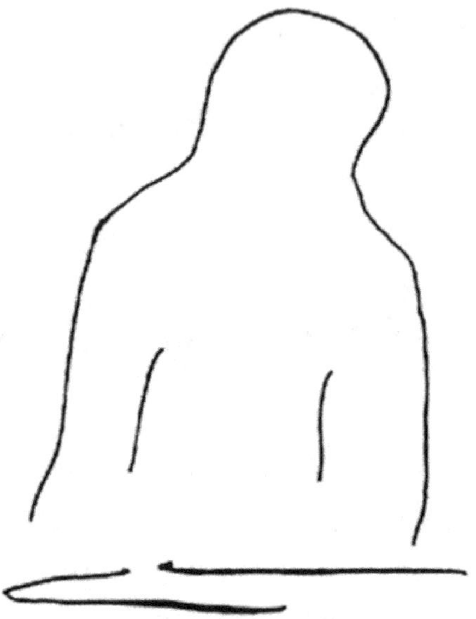

Spirit entities, like the alleged "Shadow People," are sometimes associated with UFO phenomena. Betty Jean Klem's facsimile of the "dark, shadowy, featureless creature" that scared her out of her wits during the UFO encounter. Sketch obtained from the files of the late premier ufologist, Timothy Green Beckley (1947-2021), a.k.a., "Mr. UFO," as published in his column, "On the Trail of the Flying Saucers," *Flying Saucers* magazine, Amherst, Wisconsin, Issue No. 67. December 1969.

Later Findings in the Presque Isle Case

Douglas Tibbets was taken to Hamot Hospital in Erie on the day after the incident where he was diagnosed with a slightly elevated temperature and an "inflammation of the throat."

Anita Haifley, the young woman who remained in the back seat of the car with her two children, and who initially reported that she did not see the monster sighted by her friend Betty Jean Klem in the front seat, nevertheless reported that for three weeks after the incident, she was plagued with nightmares about being attacked by a very tall, dark creature. When Dr. Schwarz tried to question her about the incident and the subsequent nightmares, Haifley unfortunately refused to discuss the matters with him.

Erie Patrolman Gagnon, after his visit to the site, became ill upon returning home later that evening, also suffering with similar maladies as diagnosed for Tibbets in the Erie hospital. Gagnon explained that he had previously suffered no such illness as the one he experienced following his visit to the UFO landing site.

PSYCHIATRIC ANALYSIS BY DR. B. E. SCHWARZ

According to the prominent psychiatrist, Dr. Berthold Eric Schwarz: "On 5 and 6 January 1968, Miss Klem and Mr. La Belle,[12] the fourth witness, were examined psychiatrically. Their accounts of the events and specific chronology were entirely similar to the many published accounts and other records in Chief Dascanio's files. Miss Klem and Mr. La Belle, before the Presque Isle episode, had been nonbelievers in UFOs; and neither of them had read more in the popular press than perhaps the average person. Interrogation of three of Miss Klem's friends of several years' standing, as well as her husband,[13] supported her reputation for truthfulness. Miss Klem seemed to be above average intelligence. She answered questions in a straightforward, open way. She appeared to be healthy, her only defect being myopia, which was completely corrected with glasses. There was no evidence for any past or present sociopathic behavior, or neurotic character traits. In the presence of her husband, she was induced into a hypnotic trance; and the salient details of the alleged UFO experience were fully confirmed. There were never any variations in her account."[14]

---

[12] Dr. Schwarz includes Gerald La Belle as the fourth witness to this event, insofar as he reported seeing the UFO flash across the sky while he was walking to Erie to obtain help in moving his stuck automobile out of the sand dune.

[13] She was married in 1967, one year after the incident.

[14] Dr. Berthold Eric Schwarz, "UFOs: Delusion or Dilemma," *Medical Times* (Stroudsburg, Pennsylvania: Romaine Pierson Publications, Vol. 86, No. 10, October 1968), 967-982.

Unidentified Submarine Objects (USOs) are frequently sighted both descending into and emerging from Lake Erie. Artwork source: http://farfuturehorizons.blogspot.com/

ANCILLARY REPORTS POINT TO "SAUCER NEST" IN OR NEAR ERIE, PENNSYLVANIA, OR UNIDENTIFIED SUBMARINE OBJECT (USO) BASE UNDERNEATH LAKE ERIE

On Wednesday, 3 August 1966, the *Erie Daily News* published an article concerning reports of UFO activity to the south of Erie, Pennsylvania, that had been investigated by some of their reporters. One rural couple denied the *Daily News* permission to reveal their names in any forthcoming stories insofar as "they are already suffering because of their having told neighbors about the sighting." According to the newspaper report, the couple stated that they had observed a cigar-shaped object "shortly after the Fourth of July." The *Daily News* article declared that their news desk received numerous reports during the prior two weeks of a similar type of UFO in the vicinity of Erie and also out over the lake, thus lending credibility to the anonymous couple's account.

Apparently, the plethora of UFO sightings in the area caught the attention of United States Air Force personnel. One gentleman from Erie claimed that an Air

Force investigator visited his neighborhood after several calls were made from him and neighbors concerning the sighting of the cigar-shaped UFO. After checking out the UFO report, the military investigator "warned people to stay away from the object, if it should reappear."

Gabriel Green (1924-2001), the president of a civilian UFO research group in Los Angeles, California, the Amalgamated Flying Saucer Clubs of America (AFSCA), asked some of his organization's members in the Erie, Pennsylvania, area to check out the sightings and provide him with a report for later publication in the pages of their group's official monthly organ, *UFO International.*

What Green learned from the AFSCA investigators was that, "Erie residents have been seeing strange things in their skies for several years. On 15 May 1964, Mrs. Richard Gross said that her two boys noticed a strange object in the sky as they were preparing for bed. Another young boy sighted a 'chrome thing that went put-put' near his home in Kearsarge, a township in Erie County. An anonymous individual called the *Daily News* office to report a tripod-shaped craft landing at a picnic area near Erie."

From all of this data, Green concluded that, "There may be a flying saucer 'nest' somewhere near Erie."

Marcus Lowth, one of ufology's leading lights when it comes to the investigation of unidentified submarine objects (USOs) or unidentified underwater objects (UUOs), as well as numerous other types of paranormal phenomena, has cataloged hundreds of sightings of strange lights and craft emerging from, or descending into the seas, oceans, and lakes around the world. Some USO researchers and investigators, like Lowth, even claim that there are underwater alien bases present in the vicinity of the locales where these aquatic sightings have occurred.[15]

Lowth notes a unique case from Erie documented in the 2011 book *Eerie Erie: Tales of the Unexplained from Northwest Pennsylvania* by Robin Swope (Charleston, South Carolina: History Press), that examines and investigates numerous Mutual UFO Network (MUFON) reports. Many of these reports speak of USOs seen "crashing" into the water of Lake Erie. The incident in the book that caught Lowth's attention took place in 1988 and alleged that a strange craft landed on the lake

---

[15]   Marcus Lowth, "Alleged Underwater Alien UFO Bases," Stillness in the Storm, 2 February 2020, https://stillnessinthestorm.com/2020/02/10-alleged-underwater-alien-ufo-bases/ (Accessed 4 September 2023).

when it was iced over. The landing was witnessed by Sheila and Henry Baker of Erie, Pennsylvania, who filed a report with the local Coast Guard. As the mysterious craft landed, there were strange creaking and cracking sounds heard coming from the ice as well as a series of blue and red lights being emitted from the craft itself. There also appeared to be several strange triangular objects that were deployed from the USO as it was descending. These triangles moved purposely around in all directions along the iced over surface of the lake. Suddenly, the sounds on the ice stopped, and the craft and the mysterious triangles vanished. Both Lowth and Swope suggested that the main USO and its ejected probes had indeed found their way below the ice and under the water.

My friend, William Dale Harder, the director of the North Coast Aerial Phenomena Project (NCAPP) in Cleveland, Ohio, is also of the opinion that there is a saucer base under Lake Erie due to the significant amount of USO reports coming in and out of Lake Erie waters in the Greater Cleveland area his organization consistently receives and investigates.

OTHER UFO REPORTS FROM ERIE AND NORTHWEST PENNSYLVANIA

APRO Pennsylvania State Section investigators also collected other UFO reports from Erie and the northwest Pennsylvania area taking place around the same date as Betty Jean Klem's encounter with the UFO and shadow creature. These reports were published in the September-October 1966 issue of the *A.P.R.O. Bulletin* (Tucson, Arizona). A brief summary of the UFO flap follows:

On the evening of Friday, 29 July 1966, at approximately 8:30 p.m., a witness who wished to remain anonymous told an APRO investigator that he had seen a six to eight-foot-long silver object passing over Erie, Pennsylvania at an estimated speed of 300 miles per hour.

On the same evening, another anonymous witness claims that have discovered a series of "three-toed footprints" outside of his Belle Vernon, Pennsylvania, residence, which is about 120 miles south of Erie. The unusual prints measured six inches long by six inches wide.

And on the following day, 30 July, a staff photographer for the *New Castle News* of New Castle, Pennsylvania, about 75 miles south of Erie, photographed an "angular flying object" quite similar to the description of the UFO provided by Tibbets on the evening of the 31 July.

Even on the very night of the Tibbets-Klem encounter, at around 10:30 p.m., an Erie doctor living about one mile south of Presque Isle, near the coast of Lake Erie, reported seeing a "circular path of orange light about the size of a baseball (as if held at arm's length) travelling at a high rate of speed at an estimated altitude of 500 to 1,000 feet."

At 1:00 a.m. on 1 August, an anonymous witness also observed a bright light over Lake Erie for a duration of some 90 minutes.

RETURN OF THE SAME CREATURE?

To top everything off, at around 5:30 a.m. on Wednesday, 3 August 1966, an "unusual creature" was reportedly seen on the streets of Erie, Pennsylvania, by a female witness who wished to remain anonymous, but who, nevertheless, agreed to be interviewed by the world-renowned paranormal investigator, John A. Keel,[16] the author of many books on cryptids, ghosts, monsters and UFOs. Keel's report to APRO states that the woman experiencer was awakened that morning by the barking of neighborhood dogs. Upon looking out her bedroom window to see what all the commotion was about, she saw what she described as a "human-shaped being about five-feet, six-inches tall." She further noted that, "It was clothed in yellow jacket and yellow trousers, with no discernable pockets, belts or other features. The head was huge and moon-shaped and when seen from the side, the back of its head appeared to be flat. This head was covered with straggly brown hair of a muddy color. The creature had very big shoulders and a slender build. It moved with a still, jerky, mechanical motion, holding its arms close to its sides. They (the arms) did not move at all. Its legs did not bend at the knees. He moved like a mechanical, wind-up toy."

---

[16]   For a detailed description of the life and work of John A. Keel (1930-2009), see Raymond A. Keller, "Chapter 6: Evolution of an Enlightened Ufologist" in *Flying Saucers: From Venus They Come* (Terra Alta, West Virginia: Headline Books, 2022), 104-107.

While the local dogs were barking and nipping at the creature's heels, it did not seem to be bothered by them. Our witness then, being quite frightened, decided to wake up her husband, calling him to the bedroom window. When he looked outside, however, all he could see was some movement in the bushes along their property line.

The creature was also spotted again that night across from the United Oil storage tanks on West Third Street in Erie, also walking stiffly and out of sight behind some of the larger tanks.

THE FLAP CONTINUES

At 11:45 p.m., on Wednesday, 3 August 1966, Clebert Steff, an advertising department employee of the *Erie Times-News,* witnessed a bright flying object in the skies over Erie through binoculars displaying red and white lights. The object traveled from west to east on an estimated angle of 30 degrees. The UFO's flight path was highly erratic and no clearly defined shape could be seen. Steff did note that the UFO did not seem to move like a conventional aircraft.

Around the same time that night, an Erie electrical engineer from a large plant was getting off from his shift when he sighted some "unusual sky objects" in a seeming V-formation, which he managed to get an even better view of after getting a pair of binoculars that he kept on the back seat of his car for weekend hunting trips. Upon focusing on the UFOs with the binoculars, however, he soon discovered that it was only one object "with a V-shaped bottom, all lit up," which flew from south to north for a period of 42 seconds before "just blinking out of sight." To the electrical engineer's perspective of looking at the UFO through the binoculars, it emitted an orange glow and left no trail.

THE SCIENTIFIC BUREAU OF INVESTIGATION (SBI): LAW ENFORCEMENT OFFICERS ON THE TRAIL OF UFOs

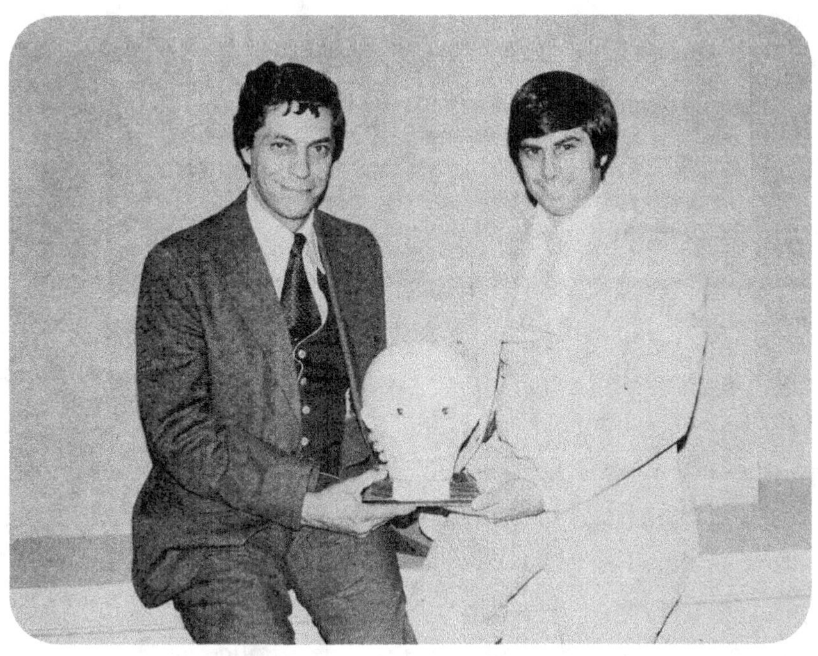

Police officers Pete Mazzola (L) and Jim Fillow (R), seen holding wax replica of the head of an extraterrestrial biological entity (EBE), organized the first UFO group primarily focusing on law enforcement personnel and their encounters with the enigmatic objects or any of their possible occupants. Headquartered in Staten Island, New York, their Scientific Bureau of Investigation (SBI) provided a more realistic alternative to then predominant Aerial Phenomena Research Organization (APRO) and National Investigations Committee on Aerial Phenomena (NICAP), groups then looking seriously into the UFO phenomenon. Photo source: *Ideal's UFO Magazine*

The decade of the 1970s was almost out when two police officers living in Staten Island, New York, Jim Fillow and Pete Mazzola, expressed disillusionment with the way that civilian UFO research organizations in the United States were dealing with the UFO phenomenon. Being law enforcement officers in the largest metropolitan area of the United States, Antonio Huneeus, ufologist and correspondent for *Ideal's UFO Magazine* (New York City, New York), paid a visit to Jim's home at 23 MacArthur Boulevard, Staten Island, New York 10312, to conduct an interview with both policemen responsible for forming a UFO research organization exclusively for fellow law enforcement officers anywhere in the world who were interested in getting to the truth behind the great mystery of UFOs. At Huneeus' initial meeting with Jim and Pete, Officer Pete Mazzola succinctly explained their reason for starting the investigative group, the Scientific Bureau of Investigation (SBI): "We are part of a new breed of ufologists, with modern-day ideas and procedures," adding that, "We feel the UFO mystery is solvable within our lifetime and we will not rest until it is solved."[17]

The two co-directors of the SBI divulged that the total number of members in their new group, at the end of 1979, after just short of one year of being in existence, was 1,236 scattered across the United States and 39 foreign countries. While their organization was formed for the benefit of informing law enforcement officials in sundry capacities about the manifold aspects of the UFO phenomenon, it wasn't restricted exclusively to law enforcement officers. Anyone with an interest in UFOs could join. However, Jim and Pete explained to Huneeus that a full 46 percent of the membership consisted of law enforcement officers working as cops, deputies, highway patrolmen, sheriffs, etc. The sizable number of such law enforcement personnel certainly set the SBI apart from other then contemporary American UFO groups, like the Aerial Phenomena Research Organization (APRO) in Tucson, Arizona, or the National Investigations Committee on Aerial Phenomena (NICAP) in Kensington, Maryland, a northern suburb of Washington, DC.

Huneeus pointed out the significance of this. "Policemen," he noted, "are not strangers to the UFO field. Both as direct witnesses and as links between the government and the public, the police have provided an invaluable service. There are

---

[17] Antonio Huneeus, "Lawmen on the Trail of UFOs: The Scientific Bureau of Investigation," *Ideal's UFO Magazine,* #10 (New York City, New York: Ideal Publishing Company, May 1980)

literally hundreds of cases involving policemen on record, one of the most famous being Lonnie Zamora's 1964 close encounter of the third kind in Socorro, New Mexico."

Officer Jim Fillow backed up Huneeus' comments when he declared, "The fact is that police officers have the highest percentage of UFO encounters of any profession." Because of this, it comes as no surprise that among law enforcement officials, there is little or no ridicule of flying saucer and UFO reports being made in any channel, official or civilian. They know that UFOs are quite real from personal experiences with them, or even their occupants. Police personnel are also professionally trained to conduct investigations in numerous areas of interest to authorities. Jim elucidated on this point: "If we can do criminal investigation, we can investigate a UFO incident. A policeman has already gone through a school and is used to getting acquainted with the figures and facts. A police officer is trained not to have an emotional involvement in an investigation. The SBI evaluates what has happened without adding anything to it, more or less as a policeman would. You don't add anything or subtract anything."

POLICE BACKGROUNDS

Going back to 1965, Both Jim and Pete had prior experience as UFO investigators for APRO, in addition to extensive training and experience in law enforcement that they have brought to their work in ufology. While they both live in Staten Island, Jim commutes to New Jersey, where he serves as a police officer; with Pete employed closer to home in New York City as a cop on a beat in addition to operating a polygraph machine at police headquarters.

Both gentlemen bring other skills to their jobs and ufology careers. Jim is a certified computer technician and Pete has achieved a Bachelor of Science degree in psychology. The two officers are also members in good standing with the American Institute of Aeronautics and Astronautics, so nobody can say that they don't know anything about outer space. Those who meet these SBI co-directors agree that they make a great team, working well together. Jim is described as "calmer and more laid back," while Pete tends to be the more "aggressive and outspoken" one. They are both married to wives who, for the most part, share their interest in all things UFO and paranormal, to the extent that they have been willing to help their husbands with all the administrative tasks in running an international organization.

PROBLEMS NOTED IN THE UFOLOGY COMMUNITY

Pete Mazzola noted that the state of ufology was dismal: "We declare that all UFO organizations of known fame are coming to a never-ending path, a dead-end. They have gotten nowhere in 33 years because of animosity among themselves."

Jim Fillow echoed these sentiments when he added, "I don't want to sound negative, but the people who work for the other organizations are working a very narrow mine field. It's the old-timers versus the new-timers. People of our age are starting to get involved, because people who have been here for 30 years have not solved the mystery. And that is what the SBI wants to do." At the time of this interview, Fillow was 30 and Mazzola 35 years of age.

GETTING STARTED

Huneeus asked Jim how the SBI got started, to which the New Jersey policeman replied, "Initially, we started through ads, mostly in law enforcement journals, stating what we wanted and how we were planning to get it. The response from police officers was tremendous."

Pete chimed in, "Of course, you are always going to have your skeptical cases, but basically cops are willing to cooperate. Jim can attest to it, that we have never been turned down by a police station. My badge is from New York, but New Jersey police reciprocate because I am a police officer." Pete has acknowledged that when it comes to investigating UFO reports, there is no doubt that police channels haven proven to be very effective. "In New Jersey, for example," Pete remarked, "if you call the police saying you saw a UFO, they send a car to the area and actually document the case. Now the file is closed to the public, but we have access to it. We get copies of every (UFO) report and follow up on them."

Both Jim and Pete made sure that the SBI established a UFO hotline for all residents of the East Coast states of New Jersey and New York. The officers proudly noted that in several cities in these two states, the SBI UFO hotline was listed in the front section of telephone books, right after the police, fire department, emergency hospitals, etc. And like APRO, the group they were most familiar with investigating members before starting their own, the SBI utilizes the services of expert technical consultants in a wide variety of specific fields with some bearing on the study of UFOs. Among these are found psychologists and psychiatrists, computer and microscope photographic analysts, laboratory personnel, operators of advanced video cassette equipment and even pilots with access to aircraft ready to taking a field investigator anywhere in the world within a 24-hour period. Of this "invisible college" working behind the scenes at the SBI, Jim and Pete remained rather secretive about divulging details. This precaution is necessary because most of these specialists are working for NASA, other government agencies or large corporations. They enjoy researching UFO cases in their spare time, but for reasons of job security and maintaining their professional stance among work associates, they prefer to remain anonymous about their off-duty careers as ufologists.

Efficient Investigations

The Co-Directors feel that immediate follow up needs to be taken by SBI field investigators receiving UFO reports coming in within their respective jurisdictions. As Pete Mazzola explained, "We formed this organization to resemble the military or a police agency. There is a definite chain of command. A chief investigator is similar to a sergeant. His is usually someone who has worked with another organization, has some experience investigating and documenting UFO cases. This person also trains the investigators and reports to a stat director who, in turn, reports to the regional director who is in charge of five states." Pete also emphasized to Huneeus that the SBI had a state director installed in each of the fifty states. And as for the qualifications to become an SBI investigator, Pete made it known that anyone over 21 years of age with a sincere interest in UFOs was welcome to apply.

"Although we don't pay our staff," noted Pete, "we do demand that they move on a case within a maximum of 48 hours. A later investigation has no use, has no value; you lose the contents. Other organizations might investigate three weeks later. We don't." Clearly, this level of efficiency in the SBI requires a sharp level of organization and coordination, the two major functions of their group.

Jim Fillow informed correspondent Huneeus about a UFO case in the New Jersey-New York-Pennsylvania Tri-State area where another UFO group "dropped the ball," so to speak. After one of that group's investigators received the UFO report, he simply let it sit on his desk for over one year; and at the time of Huneeus interview with the SBI co-directors, the UFO incident report was still sitting on that desk, apparently untouched, unmoved, unread. Jim did not believe that any of his SBI investigators would let any report just sit there like that. "That kind of stuff makes us move fast," said Jim, adding that, "If there is any physical evidence at the site, you have to get it right away. There might also be physical evidence on the witness like a scar, burn mark or something like that."

PUBLICITY CAMPAIGN

The Co-Directors were engaged in a low-key publicity campaign designed to attract a wider membership and generate funds to expand their UFO investigative work. Pete Mazzola elaborated on this campaign: "We think that publicity can be a tremendous help in solving the UFO problem. If you don't open your mouth, nobody is going to know that you exist."

Jim Fillow also opined, "According to the Gallup Poll, 57 percent (of the American population) believes in UFOs. But how many of that 57 percent that will report a UFO is another story. We say that if you report your sighting to the SBI, we'll do a professional job."

Both Pete and Jim commented on the professionalism of the SBI being one of its greatest selling points. Unlike other UFO research organizations, when the SBI receives a UFO case where there is traceable evidence, its investigators have always gotten back to the witness(es), letting them know what has been discovered in the laboratory. Thereby the SBI has gained a sterling reputation in ufology circles and the communities in which their investigators reside. The SBI also published a monthly newsletter, the *SBI Report*, with a yearly subscription going for a mere $12. The newsletter keeps the SBI membership abreast on any changes in the organization, reviews of ongoing UFO investigations, UFO events like meetings and conferences, and related UFO and paranormal information.

UFO CONSPIRACY

Editor Pete Mazzola wrote a controversial article in the September 1979 issue of the *SBI Report* speculating on the possibility that the United States military was actively engaged in constructing and test-flying at least two types of flying saucers. The first saucer is alleged to be about 12-15 feet in diameter and the second is supposed to be some 30 feet across. Mazzola had traced this report back to the 1950s with the Air Force contracting with the Canadian AVRO Company to build the code-named VZ-9 disc-shaped craft, sometimes referred to as the AVRO disc. The construction of this disc, propelled by three Continental CAE J69 turbojets, was widely publicized by the United States Air Force. "Unfortunately," Pete pointed out, "this disc was a total failure and waste of taxpayers' money."

Frankly, the AVRO disc shown to the public looked like a cheap carnival ride, barely getting a few feet off the ground. Pete Mazzola suggested that, "The Air Force, with the help of the Army, used this craft as a diversion technique so they could test and fly a real UFO allegedly seized when it crashed in 1953 in the Southwest. Of course, as yet this assumption has never been proven, but we're working on it."

In Pete Mazzola's *SBI Report* article, he relates important information pertaining to sundry projects undertaken to replicate the advanced propulsion systems evidenced in UFO reports. Among these, we find John Searl's prototype flying saucer, his "levity disc" from the United Kingdom; the disc-shaped "Andra-Jet" of Frank Andrasevitz; the Disco-Jet under construction by a California aviation/aerospace company; the French government's secret study then underway with using the principles of electrodynamics and magnetic-hydrodynamics with respect to possible modes of UFO propulsion; and lastly, a flying saucer model developed by noted NASA rocket scientist William Clendenon, then employed at the Alabama Space and Rocket Center (ASRC). This was the first time since the mid-1950s that such UFO propulsion projects were brought to the attention of the American public, taking the subject out of the realm of science fiction and seriously considering it in a multi-disciplined scientific perspective.

SBI Co-Director Jim Fillow explained why research in possible modes of UFO propulsion was so important: "We believe that the first government able to develop a disc with the capabilities (maneuverability and speed) of a UFO will have superiority in the air, will be able to pass through radar, hover quietly and outrun anything in the sky. So, militarily speaking, a disc is probably the best weapon that you could create. If you can equip the disc with a laser beam- a technology that we already have- then you can destroy almost anything. You will have a very heavy weapon."

SBI Co-Director Jim Fillow: "So, militarily speaking, a disc is probably the best weapon that you could create. If you can equip the disc with a laser beam- a technology that we already have- then you can destroy almost anything. You will have a very heavy weapon." Flying saucer zapping death ray at group of soldiers around the base of the Washington Monument in Washington, DC, as appearing in epic science fiction movie, *Earth vs. the Flying Saucers* (Columbia Pictures, Los Angeles, California, 1956).

When it comes to the United States government's cover-up of UFO information, euphemistically called the "Cosmic Watergate" or "UFOgate," the Co-Directors were filing with various federal agencies to secure UFO-related documentation through the Freedom of Information Act (FOIA). New York attorney Peter Gersten was helping the SBI Co-Directors, along with directorates of two other private UFO organizations, Ground Saucer Watch and Citizens Against UFO Secrecy (CAUS), to accomplish this formidable task. Pete Mazzola declared that, "We want to cover the entire basic structure of the United States government, and we don't care about the consequences. We are not militant. We are not subversive. But we want to get information which we know is there." To this end, Pete Mazzola pointed out to Huneeus that he and Co-Director Jim Fillow had already filed several FOIA requests with the National Aeronautics and Space Administration (NASA), the Department of Defense (DoD), the Navy, the Air Force and the Central Intelligence Agency (CIA).

Unfortunately, they, like other concerned ufologists filing such requests, would after some elapsed time, receive the UFO files, but highly redacted, with pertinent names, locations and other facts blackened out.

PERSONAL UFO EXPERIENCES

In multimedia interviews, Pete Mazzola and Jim Fillow laughingly refer to themselves as the SBI's "Two Chief Honchos." Directing an organization dedicated to uncovering the truth about UFOs, naturally directs the question in their direction as to whether the Co-Directors have themselves seen one or more these elusive objects?

Artist's conception of UFOs sighted by U.S. Army solider Pete Mazzola in 1965 hovering over a Vietnamese rice paddy. Artwork source: ***Night Sky II*** **website.**

Pete Mazzola answered this question in the affirmative, stating that his first encounter with UFOs took place during the very beginnings of the United States Armed Forces involvement in the Vietnam War, where he served as an Army advisor. While on patrol along the central coast, his squad got pinned down in the elephant grass by the Vietcong. His comrades stayed low and hid, hoping to come up with some way to escape this predicament. Amid this conundrum, the squad members saw some unidentified bright objects rise over a rice paddy, just hovering above it. Pete radioed in the position of the objects, and from the south, American battleships got a fix on the UFOs and began a bombardment of them from afar; and simultaneously, the Vietcong began directing fire at them. The UFOs departed the area as soon as they were attacked. Neither the Americans nor the Vietcong recognized the UFOs as being friendly in nature. Prior to this event, Pete had little interest in the UFO phenomenon, but now he was hooked,[18] and that is when he became an active member of APRO.

He and his wife Elaine also sighted a V-shaped formation of a dozen UFOs fly over their home in Staten Island on New Year's Eve of 1978. "Now this is Staten Island, my home, and I was not expecting to see any UFOs here," declared Pete, adding that, "When I first told my wife, she thought I was on the brink, you know, of flipping out. Being a UFO investigator, you would think I was prepared, but I was not. I didn't have a camera loaded." Fortunately, after a wait of 40 minutes, the UFOs appeared again, but flying in the opposite direction; and Pete was able to snap one clear shot encompassing the entire formation. His photo was later analyzed in a police lab, enhancing it with a computer; and it was verified as authentically "unidentified."

Jim Fillow's first sighting of UFOs was in the company of his friend and Co-Director Pete Mazzola. "I had never seen one before," said Jim, also noting that, "I had started very skeptically, initially." He then went on to explain that he and Pete were driving through North Jersey when they saw "two beautiful gold discs." This prompted Jim to do some triangulation on them, thereby estimating that the discs were no more than half a mile away at an approximate altitude of 1,000 feet. And while Jim did have a loaded camera with him, he did not get a chance to use it. He remarked that, "I didn't want to take my eyes off the objects of for fear of losing them."

---

[18]   *The Night Sky II*, Pete Mazzola's Sighting , 29 April 2023 (Accessed 17 May 2025).

Pete Mazzola's take on the encounter backed up Jim Fillow's account: "An interesting thing happened in which we were both looking through binoculars at two different UFOs simultaneously, and only when they converged, we realized we had each been watching a different disc. It was fantastic."

PRISTINE MOTIVES

Co-Director Jim Fillow, considering all the serious work that needs to be done to put the subject of flying saucers into a proper focus, asserted that the SBI would remain steadfast in its ongoing mission of accomplishing just this. "I think the reason we got our membership over 1,200 in such a short period of time is because of the way we have handled the situation. We didn't walk in and start making jewelry, pendants and UFO T-shirts. We started legitimately and said, 'Look, we want to find out what is going on here. The phenomenon is not going to go away.' We took the bull by the horns ad faced the problem head-on."

The SBI discontinued its publication, *SBI Report*, in 1985, and the organization was disbanded following the passing of Pete Mazzola in 1987.

UNITED KINGDOM POLICE CONSTABLE'S OBSESSION WITH FLYING SAUCERS AND THEIR ALIEN OCCUPANTS

Pioneer Ufologist Police Constable Anthony (Tony) Todd (1935-2009) in November 1988 at time of his retirement from the Yorkshire, U.K. Constabulary, and 35 years of dedicated professional service in law enforcement. Photo source: *Daily Star* (London, U.K.)

As happens with so many law enforcement officers around the world who have experienced close encounters with UFOs, Police Constable Tony Dodd of the North Yorkshire Constabulary in the United Kingdom, became obsessed with awakening the public to the truth about extraterrestrials visiting Earth in their flying saucers.

Dodd's initial UFO sighting took place at 3:30 a.m. on the moonless night of Monday, 9 January 1978, when he was driving his cruiser with fellow Police Constable Alan Dale alongside him in the front seat, on patrol in the remote moors at Cononley, near Skipton. "Suddenly," said Dodd, in describing this incident to Gordon Wilkinson, a reporter for the *Daily Star* (London, United Kingdom), "there it was, a spectacular, shimmering, flying saucer hovering 100 feet over the road. It was staggering, an actual spacecraft, a magnificent flying saucer about 100 feet across and glowing with an incandescent light."[19]

Up to the night of this amazing UFO encounter, Dodd rarely paid any attention to similar reports. Since 1953, the Police Constable dutifully served the citizens in the Yorkshire North Country, upholding law and order and promoting equal justice for all under the law. With all the lawbreakers afoot, Dodd had little time for UFO reports, let alone sightings of flying saucer occupants trapsing about the country-side. Frankly, Police Constable Dodd chocked up all the hullabaloo surrounding flying saucers and extraterrestrials to the fertile imaginations of the locals caught up in the science fiction novels of Arthur C. Clarke and H. G. Wells. For the quarter century of service that he rendered to the community in his capacity as a Police Constable, Tony Dodd had gained the sterling reputation of being both a dedicated and sensible officer on the force.

In turning our attention back to Tony Dodd's initial UFO encounter, he explained to journalist Gordon Wilkinson that, "All around it (the UFO) were colored lights, looking as if they were shining from some portholes. But it made no noise. There was just an eerie silence, and then it sped away. We were flabbergasted. But it was a real spacecraft, all right. I was three years in the Royal Air Force before joining the police force, so I know how to recognize conventional aircraft."

In November of 1988, after 35 years of dedicated service, Tony Dodd retired from the Constabulary. He could now devote more of his time to ufology, and was handily elected as the Director of Investigations for the Yorkshire UFO Society.

---

[19] Gordon Wilkinson, "Aliens are Tony's Life," *Daily Star* (London, UK), 27 February 1989.

Dodd's residence was in the Dales, an area noted for frequent UFO sightings; of which the retired constable had many while participating in night-time sky watches with other Yorkshire UFO Society members. At the start of 1989, there were some 300 members of the Yorkshire UFO Society, and nearly all of them physically able had gone out on the sky watches, bringing with them high-powered telescopes, cameras and Geiger counters. "On one occasion (of a sky watch)," said Dodd, "I actually flashed my car lights at a space craft and it signaled back to me."

The *Daily Star* reporter Gordon Wilkinson was curious as to why some Yorkshire UFO Society members would bring Geiger counters out to a sky watch or UFO investigation. Tony Dodd replied with a very technical explanation, but basically summed it up by pointing out that flying saucer landing sites frequently emit radiation long after the crafts have departed the area. The radiation was the residue from the crafts' power supplies.

OTHER UFO HOT SPOTS

It wasn't just the Dales that was a hot spot for UFO activity, but the whole of the Yorkshire North Country. Tony Dodd added that, "The area around Carleton Moor has been visited by aliens many times. There are other hot spots around the country, such as Warminster, near Salisbury Plain. The UFOs are there to be seen if people take the time and patience to search for them. There are about a thousand sighted in Britain every year."

That the Salisbury Plain turned out to be one of the biggest UFO hot spots in the United Kingdom comes as no surprise to ufologists worldwide, for that is where the ancient Stonehenge monument can be found. Stonehenge is a prehistoric megalithic structure smack dab in the middle of the Salisbury Plain in Wiltshire, England, two miles west of Amesbury. It consists of an outer ring of vertical sarsen standing stones, each around 13 feet high, seven feet wide, and weighing around 25 tons. They are topped by connecting horizontal lintel stones that are held in place with mortise and tenon joints, a feature unique among contemporary monuments. Ancient astronaut theorists speculate that Stonehenge may have been constructed as a landing marker for incoming flying saucers.

Developing Thoughts on the Alien Presence

Once he retired from the Constabulary in1988, in Tony Dodd's new capacity as the Yorkshire UFO Society Director of Investigations, he began to compile a computer registry for all the UFO sightings throughout the entire United Kingdom. Dodd explained that, "Though we are a Yorkshire Society, our members are all over the country. Therefore, as soon as Dodd becomes aware of a freshly reported UFO sighting taking place anywhere in the United Kingdom, he immediately dispatches one of his regional investigators to the scene. From all the hundreds of UFO reports that the retired constable has reviewed or personally investigated over the years, he has advanced two theories:

1. "The aliens obviously have some reason for keeping to remote areas. Maybe they don't want to panic people. 90 percent of sightings are in rural areas."
2. "The aliens obviously are of a highly advanced intelligence and could make themselves known to us whenever they like."

Uncooperative Government

To get the up-till-now uncooperative government of the United Kingdom to take some action in revealing the truth about the UFO phenomenon, retired Police Constable Tony Dodd declared that, "We (the members of the Yorkshire UFO Society) are determined to compile so much evidence on UFOs that the government will finally acknowledge that the aliens are here. Governments around the world have known about the aliens for many years; but for their own reasons, they refuse to let us know the truth.

"When I was on the force, I dared not speak out too much for fear of being branded a 'crank.' But now I can come forward. What I want now is feedback from the public. Those who have had close encounters can contact me on the UFO hotline (0756-752216). All calls will be dealt with in confidence.

"Many policemen, and others who are out and about at night, have seen UFOs. But they are frightened of being ridiculed if they report them. There will be many more people in the air industry and scientific community with evidence. It's high time they came forward and the truth about the aliens was finally acknowledged. Newspapers and TV stations have plagued me for years for interviews. But I know the *Daily Star* has always taken an interest in the UFO phenomenon and it is fitting that the paper should tell my story."

Hypnotic Clues in UFO Abductions

The Yorkshire UFO Society Director of Investigations came to believe that in some of the cases that he and his team have checked out, the abduction of Britons by extraterrestrials emerged as a common motif. Once taken aboard the alien spacecraft, the abducted humans were thoroughly given a medical examination. Retired Police Constable Tony Dodd also surmised that the memories of the abductees in some of these episodes seemed to have been at least partially erased. But thanks to hypnosis by qualified professionals, those individuals who sense that they may have been abducted by extraterrestrials due to time loss that they could not account for, can still unlock their memories of the UFO experience.

Tony Dodd told reporter Wilkinson about a 41-year-old housewife from Colne in Lancaster who was snatched from bed even while her husband was sleeping next to her. Under hypnosis, this female abductee's memory of experiencing a three-hour ordeal at the hands of three silver-suited spacemen who examined her on some kind of operating table aboard a flying saucer.

Tony Dodd also informed Wilkinson of two friends from Keighley in Yorkshire who experienced 45-minute memory losses after driving together through the moors. And there was a 32-year-old Halifax woman who claimed that she was engulfed in a ball of brilliant light and beamed up into a flying saucer where she was medically examined by robots under the command of humanoid-appearing extraterrestrials. In both cases, Dodd reported that the UFO experiences were able to regain their memories of these episodes while placed under hypnosis by qualified professionals on loan to the Yorkshire UFO Society from law enforcement agencies.

ARGENTINE POLICE OFFICER EMBROILED IN "MISSING TIME" EXTRATERRESTRIAL ABDUCTION CASE

At left, La Pampa Province, Argentina, Motorcycle Patrolman Sergio Pucheta at age 31, following encounter with flying saucer and its mysterious occupants in March 2006. At right, Pucheta later recalls his encounter in American television interview. Photo credits: National Broadcasting Corporation

Sergio Pucheta is a Police Corporal who works in La Ciudad de General Pico (The City of General Pico) at La Pampa Province Police Detachment headquartered there. From approximately 10 p.m. on Thursday, 2 March 2006, extending to 4:30 p.m. on the following day, Pucheta claims that he was abducted by extraterrestrials and taken aboard their flying saucer for a complete physical examination, before he was finally released.

Police Corporal Sergio Pucheta had been a distinguished member of the force for eight years, with his last two years prior to the UFO incident serving in the Anti-Cattle Rustling Squad of the Anti-Theft Division (*La División Anti-Abigeato*). In this capacity, his patrols encompassed the rural districts of Dorila, Speluzzi and Trebolares. This area is situated in the center of La Pampa Province, and geographically in the very center of the Republic of Argentina.

Of his close encounter of the third kind (CE3), Police Corporal Sergio Pucheta later informed a correspondent from *El Diario de La Pampa* newspaper in Santa Rosa, La Pampa Province, Argentina, that, "I was driving a Honda 25cc motorcycle belonging to the Anti-Cattle Rustling Squad; and when I reached the wilderness area we call 'Las Cañas,' I saw a red light like that of a car. When I finally arrived at the site of the light's flickering, the light vanished. Then I got off my motorcycle to see if I could hear any noises. When I got back on my motorcycle and was about to put on my helmet, the red light appeared in front of my body. It was as if the light was scanning my entire body."[20]

While the bright red light remained stationary in front of Police Corporal Pucheta's face, he expressed the feeling that, "It sort of hypnotized me." He also explained, "I could only move my hands, nothing else. I could not move the rest of my body. The light was moving all over my body." When this red light rose above his head, however, Pucheta remarked that, "It caused me a considerable head and eye ache."

With the light not scanning his body anymore, Police Corporal Pucheta regained feeling and movement in his legs. Therefore, he attempted to escape, making a dash for cover in the nearby woods. In the rush to get out of this area, the officer abandoned his service pistol, walkie-talkie, and cell phone. About half an hour after Officer Pucheta radioed in his report of the UFO, when the site of this encounter was visited by investigators, they recovered these items on the highway alongside

---

[20] Wednesday, 8 March 2006 edition.

Pucheta's abandoned motorcycle, but found the service pistol totally dismantled and all of Pucheta's stored telephone numbers erased, except for the last call he had made back to the La Pampa Province Police Detachment Headquarters requesting backup.

Police Corporal Sergio Pucheta when he was discovered along a rural road in La Pampa Province, Argentina, following his abduction by UFO occupants in March 2006. Photo source: *La Capital* **newspaper, Rosario, Argentina**

When Officer Pucheta was found on the following day at 4:30 p.m., he appeared to be numb and curled up in a fetal position along a rural road in the village of Quemu Quemu, some 20 kilometers away from the area where he disappeared. Regarding this location where he was rescued by fellow police officers, Pucheta declared that, "I was there from 8:00 in the morning until past 4:00 in the afternoon, sitting and waiting in a place where no one ever came by." The officer explained why he could not move away from this site: "My feet were paralyzed and I was numb."

From Quemu Quemu, Officer Pucheta was transported by ambulance to the Gobernador Centeno Hospital in the City of General Pico, where he remained until noon on Monday, 6 March 2006. The reporter from *El Diario de La Pampa* was not able to interview him until the following day, when he had returned to his home at the intersection of 104th and 25th Streets in General Pico, where his pregnant wife and in-laws had been anxiously awaiting him. When the correspondent queried Officer Pucheta about his close encounter, he had no recollection of taking apart his service pistol or erasing any of his stored telephone numbers.

While running away from the UFO in the middle of a rural field, however, Officer Pucheta remembered having been pursued by two mysterious entities. He could not shake them off. "They were always behind me!" he declared to the reporter from *El Diario de La Pampa*. The beings that chased him were "levitated," according to Pucheta's report, and "seemed to be of a smaller stature than most humans." He also took note that, "They were somewhat transparent, with large heads and clear red eyes. The eyes were very red."

Police Corporal Pucheta also recalled observing another strange entity when he reached the edge of a cornfield. "At a distance of 10 meters," the officer explained, "I saw a large figure that appeared to be chewing the corn cobs and seemed to be breaking something. I felt scared and stood there, staring at it. It was getting closer and closer, and that's when I heard a voice in my head telling me, 'Either you go forward or backward.' Then I stood there thinking for a moment, and then walked right past the figure. Then the fear sort of left me, at that moment."

The reporter wondered if this entity might have been some kind of wild animal, but Officer Pucheta insisted that it wasn't. "No," he said, "because it was taller than me and much larger." The officer confided that he had a gut feeling that it was an extraterrestrial or ultra-dimensional being associated with the UFO and the other two entities that pursued him. Some ufologists like Stan Gordon of the Mutual UFO Network in Pennsylvania, have correlated reports of Bigfoot entities with UFO sightings in certain "vortex areas," such as some of the more remote sections along the Chestnut Ridge in Southwest Pennsylvania.[21] Your authors speculate that this large entity in Police Corporal Pucheta's case may be a Bigfoot.

---

[21] Dr. Raymond A. Keller, II, and Fred Saluga, *Pennsylvania in the Paranormal Vortex* (Terra Alta, West Virginia: Headline Books, 2025), 64, 65.

Throughout his UFO experience, Patrolman Pucheta remarked that he attained a heightened degree of awareness with respect to prominent lifetime memories leading up to the point of his abduction. He thought intently about his family, his wife and his yet unborn child. "I began remembering everything I had ever been through since childhood. That was the loveliest thing that happened to me."

Officer Pucheta still remains unsure if the entities transported him to any more distant locales, but he has vague recollections of "floating in the air and passing over some young bull calves in a field."

On the negative side, Police Corporal Pucheta said that, "I still feel very afraid about going out at night. The entities told me telepathically that they would not have any qualms about abducting me again or any fellow officer who also travels alone."

Leading up to Police Corporal Sergio Pucheta's abduction, residents and police officers throughout La Pampa Province experienced more than their fair share of UFO encounters, with thousands of "mysterious red lights" reported since the beginning of January 2006. In early February, another officer on the force in General Pico filmed a UFO in the approximate area where Sergio Pucheta encountered the entities. The UFO video showed a round light apparently rotating on its axis. Officers from the Argentine Ministry of Defense requisitioned the UFO video immediately after Police Corporal Pucheta was reported as "missing." And in mid-February, Officer Pucheta pointed out that, "A fellow officer was driving along the access road to Agustoni and saw a light in the middle of the road. He thought it was a car and flashed his headlights at it, but the light wouldn't budge. When he was about to overtake it, the light moved from one side to another and flew straight up."

HUNT COUNTY RESIDENTS AND DEPUTIES REPORT UFO IN SKIES OVER THE LONE STAR STATE

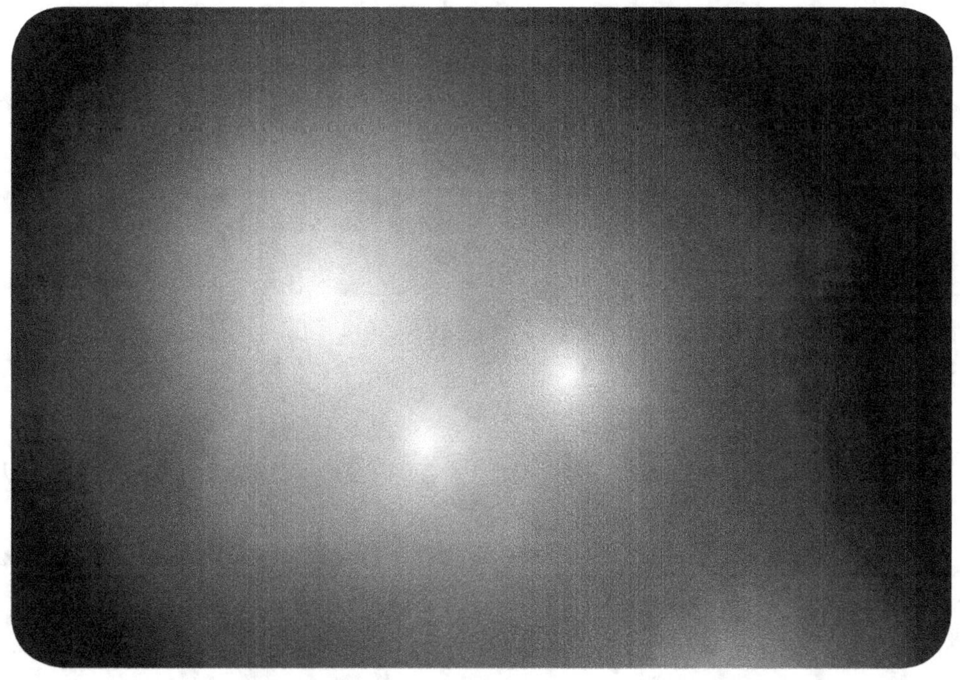

Glowing spheres such as these photographed over Round Rock, Texas, in early September 2022 have frequently been seen traversing the skies of the Lone Star State. Photo source: https://nexusnewsfeed.com/

During the last weekend of February 2009, no one in Hunt County, Texas, was sure with any degree of accuracy as to just what had appeared in the clear night skies overhead. At least one civilian and three uniformed law enforcement officers reported seeing a UFO north of Greenville around 9:20 p.m. on Saturday, 28 February 2009. And according to the Hunt County Sheriff Randy Meeks, other UFO sightings were reported in the vicinity of The Colony over in adjacent Denton County.

The first report of a UFO came with a telephone call to the Hunt County Sheriff Department, with Sheriff Randy Meeks answering it. The call came at 9:20 p.m. on Saturday, 28 February 2009, from a frightened woman who lives along the Farm-to-Market Road 2358, not far from the Webb Hill Country Club. Meeks explained that, "She said it was hovering over her house. It was really bright. Then it went dim; then it went bright again. Then it moved away. It was moving from that area toward Dallas."

The Sheriff noted that the witness declared that the UFO did not sound anything like an aircraft, at least a conventional one. It didn't sound like a helicopter, either. It sounded more like a mass of bees "buzzing in and around a hive." The observer also informed the Sheriff that one of her cousins, living in The Colony, also reported a similar aerial phenomenon taking place that night. The UFO witness was frightfully aware that she and her cousin were not alone out there that night.

Once Sheriff Randy Meeks got on the radio to request that any available deputies check out the UFO report, three of them answered his call, all reporting that they could see the UFO from their current position. One of these deputies, in the Campbell area, not far from the Webb Hill Country Club, drove out to the site of the original UFO spotting. He got a better view of the object, describing it as some type of "glowing sphere." The other two deputies just reported seeing a "bright light" that they could offer no logical explanation for.

In an interview with staff writer Brad Kellar from the Greenville, Texas, *Herald-Banner* newspaper, Sheriff Randy Meeks stated that he had followed up on the UFO reports by personally checking with L-3 Communications Integrated Systems, a local defense contractor operating out of Majors Field Municipal Airport in Greenville to see if any pilots, ground controllers, airfield personnel or radar operators had seen or detected any UFOs that night or at any other time(s) during the weekend. "They (the Municipal Airport employees) said that they did not have anything up in the air at the times that any of the UFO sightings occurred."[22]

---

[22] Brad Kellar, "UFO visits Hunt County-mysterious object seen by resident, deputies," *Herald-Banner,* Greenville, Texas, 02 March 2009.

MEXICAN POLICE IN UFO CHASE NEAR UNITED STATES BORDER

Martin Ruelas, the Mexicali Police Department Western Sector Supervisor, seen here being interviewed by local journalist Juan Galván, was the first officer to arrive on site at the airport to see the object quickly move out of the area. Photo source: *Voz de la Frontera* (*Voice of the Border*) newspaper, Mexicali, B.C., Mexico, 24 January 2012

During the early evening of Monday, 23 January 2012, a slew of UFO reports was received telephonically at Mexicali Police Headquarters. The callers noted that the object, first spotted hovering over the Mexicali Airport, displayed "intense white lights, and was also emitting blue and yellow flashes." Public safety crisis responders at the airport (C-4 personnel) manning air traffic safety cameras managed to initiate at 7:49 p.m. a taped recording of the UFO, seen as an inset in the photo above. With all the excitement generated in the neighborhoods near the airport and the expressed concern of the airport safety responders, Mexicali police were dispatched to the airport.

Martin Ruelas, the Western Sector Supervisor, was the first to arrive on the scene and see with his own eyes the mysterious object, which had already begun to move quickly out of the area. Officer Ruelas described the UFO as a "sizable round object with visible blue and yellow flashes." He also noted that, "It moved up, down and sideways at very high speeds, vanishing from sight after heading southwest from the Mexicali Valley."

Another Mexicali police officer, Alejandro Monreal Noriega, the General Commander of Patrols in the Directorate of Municipal Public Safety in Mexicali, informed local media that the first reports of the UFO came from people living in the vicinity of the airport. Hundreds of phone calls were received on the 066-emergency line from witnesses to the presence of a UFO over the airport. After hovering over the airport, the UFO flew at dizzying speeds out to the Marán Industrial Park[23] to the northwest and then cutting sharply on to the Rivera Campestre District a few miles to the southwest, whence it made a bee-line out of sight beyond the western horizon. Deputy Commander H. Medina from Mexicali's Southern District also witnessed the UFO, but noted that, "It was moving too fast and impossible to follow, as it changed direction suddenly and disappeared in the western sky." Officer Medina's testimony confirmed those of the others in the Mexicali Police Department, at least insofar as its flight path.

With all the UFO reports coming in, a chase of the object by patrolmen put on alert ensued throughout the Mexicali Valley that night. But insofar as the UFO was moving so fast and kept changing its direction, as soon as the object vanished from the sight of one officer, the nearest patrolmen further along its flight path was informed to continue the pursuit. Nevertheless, it became impossible to track the

---

[23]   Now known as the Nicoya Industrial Park.

UFO once it passed beyond the western boundaries of the city and proceeded out over the desert.

The General Commander of Patrols Alejandro Monreal Noriega did declare to Juan Galván, a reporter for the Mexicali newspaper, *La Voz de la Frontera* (*Voice of the Border*),[24] that "Consultations were made with airport authorities and the Secretariat of National Defense (SEDENA) in Mexico City, as well as their counterparts in the United States, and they are awaiting more information on the subject from us. SEDENA will also dispatch investigators to Mexicali insofar as the UFO seemed to run along an east-to-west trajectory parallel with the United States border, thus making these reports a matter of national security."

---

[24] Juan Galván, "Police Engage in UFO Chase," Tuesday, 24 January 2012 edition, *La Voz de la Frontera*, Mexicali, B.C., Mexico.

APPENDIX A

FEDERAL BUREAU OF INVESTIGATION (FBI) REPORTS ON PROMINENT CONTACTEE GEORGE ADAMSKI (1891-1965)

George Adamski's public statements on the extraterrestrial presence in America provoked FBI interest in his case.

In photo at upper right, Adamski pointing to one of his photos of extraterrestrial spaceships, explains their motive power, speeds and maneuverability to interviewer Long John Nebel of WOR Radio, 710 AM, on the *Party Line* radio program heard nightly in the late 1950s over 25 states and the eastern half of Canada.

FEDERAL BUREAU OF INVESTIGATION: ON THE TRAIL OF THE FLYING SAUCERS

The government agency with the longest involvement with ongoing research into the appearance of flying saucers in our skies, landing or crashing here on Earth, as well as the occupants who pilot these strange craft and the people who report meetings with them, is the Federal Bureau of Investigation (FBI). At least since the UFO flap of 1947 and the crash of a f lying saucer in the vicinity of Roswell, New Mexico, FBI agents have been hot on the trail of the flying saucers. That the federal government was concerned about flying saucers and the contactees' involvement with them for so long has been well known in ufology circles. Many times, visits by federal agents of the FBI and other intelligence networks left the UFO experiencer with the impression that he or she had just been raked over the coals by the mysterious "men in black," or "MIBs," whose existence was first made known in the case of Albert K. Bender and his International Flying Saucer Bureau (IFSB), one of the first civilian organizations checking out UFO sightings and occupant reports from around the world.

George Adamski, who had been contacted countless times by FBI and other federal agents, came to collectively refer to these minions as the Silence Group. Public clamor about the government's probing of various civilian groups, ranging from the Black Panther Party for Self Defense all the way to UFO investigative groups like Gabriel Green's Amalgamated Flying Saucer Clubs of America (AFSCA), headquartered at first in Los Angeles but later moved out to Yucca Valley, California, prompted cries for greater disclosure. Many objecting to such extensive federal involvement in private groups, whether they any of them are political, religious or scientific, or even a combination of these, were now demanding to know the full extent to which the very Constitution's Bill of Rights may have been violated during these federal investigations.

To at least minimally address this issue, the 89th Congress passed the Freedom of Information Act (FOIA), 5 U.S.C.§552, a federal freedom of information law that allows for the full or partial disclosure of previously unreleased information and documents controlled by the United States government. The FOIA defines various federal agency records as being subject to disclosure, outlines mandatory disclosure procedures and grants nine exemptions to the statute. The FOIA was reluctantly signed into law by President Lyndon B. Johnson on 4 July 1966, and went into effect on 5 July of the following year.[25] So while ufologists were able to successfully petition for and gain some records detailing the federal government's intrusion into their individual or group activities with regard to researching the phenomenon, that the federal government allowed the agency under the magnifying glass of public scrutiny to retain numerous exemptions to the FOIA meant that the full extent of such federal intrusions could not be fully ascertained. In the case of George Adamski, however, we find quite an extensive cache of information in the FBI files alone, dating back to 1952. Most of this data originated from the FBI's San Diego field office. Of course, there may even be more information available on Adamski from the FBI's integrated network of offices, but because of the exemptions allowed the organization by the FOIA in retaining exclusive access to information pertinent to national security concerns we may most likely never come to review it. Here are some important exerts from the FBI's own files on George Adamski, presented in chronological order:

28 May 1952, Letter from field agent in San Diego, California office to Director, FBI:

(DELETION) advised that when ADAMSKI left the group for a brief period, one of the women working in the café came over and entered into the conversation. She stated that some of our servicemen who stopped there to have drinks during World War II and subsequent thereto, told "Professor" ADAMSKI of the atrocities which they were forced to commit, murdering women and children on orders of their superior officers. (DELETION) stated that while this woman was making these statements, she exhibited a great deal of animosity against the United States, stating that the United States committed more atrocities during World War II than did the Japanese but since the Japanese were the ones who lost the war, they were the ones who were tried as war criminals.

This woman added that a friend of hers who recently returned from Russia stated he was very pleased with everything he found there. He stated to her that the people in Russia received seven tickets per month for the opera and cinema.

---

[25] "What is FOIA?" *Freedom of Information Act* website, undated, United States Department of Justice, https://www.foia. gov/about.html (Accessed 3 October 2016).

These tickets are free, being issued by the government. The woman added, "The people there (in Russia) don't have to be worrying about where their next meal is coming from. Everything is fine in Russia and in the United States we have to fight for everything we get." (DELETION) advised that ADAMSKI returned to continue his conversation stating that the United States will soon be in the same condition that Europe was in during the last war. He added that, "It is a good idea to be quiet now. Right now if you talk in favor of Communism you will be spotted as a Communist and if you talk against Communism you will be spotted by the Communist, so it's best to just shut up."

ADAMSKI stated to (DELETION) that, "The United States hasn't a chance to win the war. Russia will take over the United States." (DELETION) Valley Center, California, (DELETION) advised that ADAMSKI has lived in the vicinity for approximately ten years and is the owner of the Palomar Gardens Café. (DELETION) advised that ADAMSKI also operates a small telescope on the premises and is noted for giving lectures on "Space Ships." (DELETION) advised that ADAMSKI recently appeared on a television program in San Diego and gave a lecture on "Space Ships." (DELETION) could furnish no information concerning subversive activities on the part of ADAMSKI. (DELETION) described ADAMSKI as a very brilliant individual who gives the community the impression that he is mentally unbalanced because of his lectures on "Space Ships."

The records of the (DELETION) San Diego, examined by (DELETION) Manager, contained no information concerning ADAMSKI. The San Diego Office has opened a Security Matter case on ADAMSKI to establish whether he is sincere in his remarks pertaining to Russia and any pertinent information whih will be of value to the Cleveland Office concerning (DELETION)wa. will be forwarded to that office. RUC.

Analysis: This letter is dated before the publication of *Flying Saucers Have Landed,* so it appears that even before Adamski gained all the notoriety that came with the publication of that book in 1953, he was on the radar of at least two of the FBI's field offices, Cleveland, Ohio, and San Diego, California. This was not so much for his lectures on space ships, which were perceived as relatively eccentric but not subversive, but for the discussions going on between him, his staff and patrons at the Palomar Gardens Café concerning life and opportunities in the Soviet Union and perceived faults in the American system and way of life, generally.

In many science fiction films of the early 1950s, such as *It Came from Outer Space* (Universal-International, Universal City, California, 1953), the extraterrestrial intruders served as a veiled substitute for the alleged Soviet threat.

22 September 1952, Office Memorandum from SAC, San Diego (100-8382) to Director, FBI Subject: GEORGE A. ADAMSKI, aka; Professor George A. Adamski; George A. Adamsky SECURITY MATTER – C

Reference San Diego letter to Director, entitled (DELETION). Contrary to information furnished in referenced letter, no further investigation is being conducted concerning the captioned Subject inasmuch as the facts do not warrant a security type of investigation as prescribed by recent Bureau instructions. The following is the result of the background investigation conducted by the San Diego Office:

(DELETION) San Diego, reflect the subject was born in Hungary and was naturalized on August 25, 1915 at Philadelphia, Pennsylvania. The Subject's naturalization certificate number is 577095. The following is the subject's description as taken (DELETION):

Born: March 12, 1883, in Autrics, Hungary.

Height: 5'7"

Weight: 165

Hair: light

Eyes: Blue

Social Security #: 561-34-1686

Relative: Wife- VICTORIA K. ADAMSKI

Residence: Palomar Café (5 miles east of Rincon, California)

Occupation: Café owner, amateur astronomer

The records of DIO, 11th Naval District and the records of the Office of Special Investigations, San Diego, contained no information concerning the Subject. CTG:htw

CC: Cleveland (100-18743) Dallas Los Angeles SD 100-8382

22 September 1952 Office Memorandum to Director, FBI (PAGE TWO)

Confidential National Defense Informants of the San Diego Office were contacted and no information concerning the Subject was furnished. The Office of Special Investigations, San Diego, has been advised concerning the Subject's lectures on "Space Ships" and "Flying Saucers." Copies of this letter are being furnished to the Cleveland, Dallas and Los Angeles Offices, because these offices have received previous communications concerning the Subject. **Analysis:** It has been four months since the last known inquiry, but information on Adamski continued to be collected and reports continued to be sent to the Director's office with copies dispatched to the Cleveland office. In this memorandum, however, we note that offices in Dallas and Los Angeles were added to the growing list of recipients for Adamski information with a rationale given that these added offices, in addition to the Cleveland office, had received prior communications of an unspecified nature regarding George Adamski and his activities in their areas. Pertinent personal information, including Adamski's Social Security number and Naturalization Certificate data, are included in the growing file. The San Diego official writing this report is of the opinion that no further investigation of Adamski is warranted; and he so recommends this to J. Edgar Hoover, the Director. However, the San Diego FBI office takes the initiative of informing the San Diego Office of Special Investigations about Adamski's lectures on space ships and flying saucers, most likely if Adamski might inadvertently be stumbling into an area of national security concerns.

28 January 1953, Office Memorandum from SAC, San Diego (100-8382) to Director, FBI Subject: GEORGE ADAMSKI, was., (APPEARS TO HAVE BEEN WHITED OUT), SECURITY MATTER – C

On January 12, 1953, (DELETED) OSI, received a telephone call from a friend, name unknown, of ADAMSKI's, who advised ADAMSKI had in his possession a machine which could draw "flying saucers" and airplanes down from the sky. ADAMSKI's friend stated that ADAMSKI wished to see an Agent because of the possibility of sabotage. (DELETED) advised the San Diego Office of these facts on January 12, 1953. On January 12, 1953, GEORGE ADAMSKI, Palomar Gardens Café, foot of Mount Palomar, was interviewed by (DELETED) OSI, and SA (DELETED) FBI. ADAMSKI stated he had been working on "flying saucers" with two men by the names of (DELETED) and (DELETED). He further advised that on the morning of January 12, 1953, (DELETED) told him that he, (DELETED) was receiving a machine through the mail that would draw down flying saucers and airplanes.

According to ADAMSKI, this machine which had not arrived as yet, operated on the principle of "cutting magnetic lines of force." ADAMSKI stated that he had asked (DELETED) if it would draw down planes belong to the U.S., and (DELETED) had replied "Yes," in a manner which indicated he might not be friendly with the U.S. ADAMSKI stated that when he indicated his displeasure to (DELETED) about drawing U.S. planes down, that (DELETED) had become angry and he and (DELETED) had packed their belongings, piled them into (DELETED)'s car, (a green Crosley Station Wagon, bearing Wisconsin License Plates (DELETED) and headed for Los Angeles, California.

Their destination was unknown to him, according to ADAMSKI. ADAMSKI stated he further suspected (DELETED) of being disloyal to the United States because (DELETED) was a close friend of (DELETED). ADAMSKI advised that (DELETED) was interested in flying saucers and had correspondence with him and written numerous letters which indicated to him, ADAMSKI, that (DELETED) was not entirely loyal to the United States Government. ADAMSKI furnished the letters as evidence of his belief of disloyal attitude, which are enclosed to the Bureau and Cleveland.

SD 100-8382 28 January 1953, Office Memorandum to Director, FBI (PAGE TWO)

ADAMSKI advised that he had been corresponding with (DELETED) with regularity, for about one year, but advised that he did not know very much about (DELETED) due to the fact that he had never met him, and that (DELETED) never told him much about himself in his letters. ADAMSKI stated that he had received correspondence from (DELETED) at the following addresses: (DELETED), Campbell, Ohio, and (DELETED), Cleveland, Ohio. ADAMSKI advised that he had corresponded with (DELETED) since approximately March 12, 1951, and that on December 30, 1952, (DELETED) had appeared at the Palomar Gardens and told ADAMSKI that he wanted to work with him. ADAMSKI stated that (DELETED) had brought a tape recorder with him on which he had recorded the voice of (DELETED) giving some instructions and that (DELETED) had also brought some tools with him. ADAMSKI stated that (DELETED) had formerly been employed at the Oster Plant in Indiana and that he had been discharged from there.

ADAMSKI furnished the following description of (DELETED):

Age: 35 yrs
Height: 5'9"
Weight: 180 lbs.
Eyes: Blue
Hair: Blond; Sandy
Face: Narrow
Complexion: Fair
Scars: None
Race: German
Peculiarities: Smokes pipe, says "ya"-"ya"

Addresses: (DELETED), Wisconsin; (DELETED), Wisconsin; (DELETED), Wisconsin

SD 100-8382 28 January 1953, Office Memorandum to Director, FBI (PAGE THREE)

ADAMSKI advised that he had corresponded with (DELETED), starting approximately November 26, 1951, at which time (DELETED) had written a letter to him stating that he had heard ADAMSKI's story concerning space ships and wanted to exchange information concerning them. (DELETED) was formerly in the 371 5th Training Squadron, Lackland Air Force Base, San Antonio, Texas, and was discharged from military service in October, 1952. ADAMSKI stated that in November, 1952, (DELETED) appeared at his Palomar Gardens Café and stated he was (DELETED) and moved in. ADAMSKI advised that (DELETED) had formerly lectured on flying saucers at the Lackland Air Force Base and furnished the following description of (DELETED), of whom he stated he would consider to be a loyal American citizen:

Age: 23 yrs.
Height: 5'5" 49
Weight: 160 lbs.
Eyes: Brown
Hair: Black
Complexion: Olive
Scars: None
Speech: Soft Spoken

ADAMSKI further advised that on November 20, 1952, on the California Desert, at a point ten and two-tenths miles from Desert Center on the road to Parker and Needles, Arizona, that he had made contact with a space craft and had talked to a space man. ADAMSKI stated that he, (DELETED) and his wife MARY, had been out in the desert and that he and the persons with him had seen the craft come down to the earth. ADAMSKI stated that a small stairway in the bottom of the craft, which appeared to be a round disc, opened and a space man came down the steps. ADAMSKI stated he believed there were other space men in the ship because the ship appeared translucent and could see the shadows of the space men....

SD 100-8382 28 January 1953, Office Memorandum to Director, FBI (PAGE FOUR)

….ADAMSKI described the space man as being over 5' in height, having long hair like a woman's and garbed in a suit similar to the space suits or web suits worn by the U. S. Air Force Men. ADAMSKI stated that he and the space man conversed by signs and that there appeared to be a certain area around the space ship which consisted of magnetic or electric lines of force, inasmuch as when he got too close, some of the lines went through his arm and momentarily paralyzed his arm. ADAMSKI stated that he took a picture of the space ship and the space man, but the space man could evidently read his thoughts inasmuch as he motioned to him not to take the picture and when the space man left he took the "plate" with the negative on it with him.

ADAMSKI further advised that he had obtained plaster casts of the footprints of the space man and stated that the casts indicated the footprints had signs on them similar to the signs of the Zodiac.**35** On January 12, 1953, ADAMSKI advised that on December 13, 1952, the space ship returned to the Palomar Gardens and came low enough to drop the plate which the space man had taken from him, ADAMSKI, and had then gone off over the hill. ADAMSKI stated that he saw the space ship and that as the space ship was leaving, (DELETED) also took a picture of the ship. ADAMSKI stated that when he had the negatives developed at a photo shop in Escondido, California, that the negative that the space man had taken from him contained writing which he believed to be the writing of the space men. ADAMSKI furnished the writer with copies of the space writing and photographs of the space ship. (DELETED) at the Palomar Observatory, advised that he had been acquainted with ADAMSKI since 1943, at which time ADAMSKI had called himself "the Reverend ADAMSKI" and had held Easter Services in the Valley.

(DELETED) stated that in talking to ADAMSKI, ADAMSKI had told him, (DELETED), that he had a "cult" or colony at Laguna Beach, California, previous to 1943, and that he had also been interested in metaphysics and astrology.

SD 100-8382 28 January 1953, Office Memorandum to Director, FBI (PAGE FIVE)

(DELETED) further advised that Adamski claimed to have worked at Mount Palomar, but stated that ADAMSKI had never been employed at the Observatory. (DELETED) stated that ADAMSKI also claims to have been associated with (DELETED), formerly with the Observatory at Mount Palomar, but now located in Pasadena, California. (DELETED) stated that (DELETED) had known ADAMSKI for quite some time and that (DELETED)'s address was: (DELETED), Pasadena, California; Telephone: (DELETED).

(DELETED) stated he considered ADAMSKI to be more qualified in astrology than astronomy. He continued that he had never viewed any space ship and believed ADAMSKI to be an opportunist. Copies of the letters of (DELETED) and prints of the space writing and flying saucers, are being enclosed to the Bureau, for informational purposes only. Copies are also being enclosed to the Cleveland Office for any action that they may desire to take. This information is not being furnished to the U. S. Air Force inasmuch as (DELETED), OSI, was along at the time of the interview, and is cognizant of the facts contained herein.

Palomar Observatory is a center of astronomical research owned and run by California Institute of Technology (Caltech), the same institution that supplied and continues to supply most scientists employed at the Jet Propulsion Laboratory (JPL) in Pasadena, California. It was the JPL that in 1962 launched and guided the first successful probe to the planet Venus. The identity of the mysterious scientist at Mount Palomar who knew Adamski "for quite some time" remains a mystery. Photo source: https://www.tripadvisor.cn/

ADAMSKI furnished the following information concerning himself:

Born: 4-17-1891

Place: Poland

Father: JOSEPH ADAMSKI (deceased)

Mother: FRANCES ADAMSKI (deceased)

Sister: (DELETED) (phonetic)

Address: Lackawana, New York

Sister: (DELETED)

Address: Dunkirk, New York

Sister: (DELETED)

Address: Dunkirk, New York

SD 100-8382 28 January 1953, Office Memorandum to Director, FBI (PAGE SIX)

Brother: (DELETED)

Address: Lackawana, New York

Brother: (DELETED)

Address: Dunkirk, New York

Entered U.S.: 1893 through New York

1913-1916: Entered U.S. Army, 13th U.S. Cavalry, "K" Troop, Stationed at Columbus, New Mexico

Employment:

1916: Yellowstone Nat'l. Park (took charge of the park for the Government and was a painter)

1918: Went to Camp Lewis, U.S. Army, and entered Nat'l. Guard and stationed at Portland, Oregon, 9 months.

1918: Worked in Flour Mills in Portland, Oregon

1921: Came to California and worked in Concrete Business at Los Angeles, Calif.

1926: Began lecturing on philosophy

Education: Had not received college degree & title of Professor was nick-name.

Marital Status: Married; Wife: MARY ADAMSKI, nee (DELETED)

Address: Palomar Gardens Café

Children: None

Height: 5'8"

Weight: 171 lbs.

Hair: Gray

Eyes: Brown, cataract right eye; Complexion: Ruddy

Build: Medium

Scars: 3" scar on naval

Peculiarity: Well spoken; friendly; cannot pronounce "th" in speech;

SD 100-8382 28 January 1953, Office Memorandum to Director, FBI (PAGE SEVEN)

(DELETED) advised that when (DELETED), who as a matter of cooperation was preparing prints of the "Flying Saucers" for the San Diego Office, saw the prints he made the remark, "those are some of that crackpot ADAMSKI's shots – he has been in here with his pictures before." (DELETED) further advised he believed the photographs were taken by setting the camera lens at infinity, which would sharpen the background of mountains and trees and blurs the saucer, which was probably strung on a thin wire. (DELETED) advised that if the camera were set at infinity the wire would not show.

No further investigation is being conducted by the San Diego Office. This case is considered being closed.

ENCLOSURES TO BUREAU & CLEVELAND:

1 photograph of the Space Writing

2 photographs of the Space Ship

1 copy of letters from (DELETED)-C

Analysis: The confidential memorandum is significant because it depicts Adamski working with an alien technology, or at least being cognizant of such. In particular, the document references a machine "that would draw down flying saucers and airplanes" by means of "cutting magnetic lines of force." Interestingly, Nikola Tesla

(1856-1943), with his many ties to the second planet explored in *Venus Rising*,[26] was attempting to construct a similar device. Tesla inherited from his Eastern Orthodox father a deep hatred of war; and throughout the intrepid scientist's life, he sought a technological way to end warfare. Tesla was convinced that war could be converted into a "mere spectacle of machines." In 1931 Tesla announced at a press conference that he was on the verge of discovering an entirely new source of energy. And when he was asked to explain the nature of the power, he replied, "The idea first came upon me as a tremendous shock... I can only say at this time that it will come from an entirely new and unsuspected source."

Of course, the dark and ominous clouds of war were again converging on Europe. On 11 July 1934 the headline on the front page of the *New York Times* read, "TESLA, AT 78, BARES NEW 'DEATH BEAM,'" with the associated article reporting that the invention "will send concentrated beams of particles through the free air, of such tremendous energy that they will bring down a fleet of 10,000 enemy airplanes at a distance of 250 miles...." Tesla declared that the death beam would make war impossible by offering every country an "invisible Chinese wall."

Naturally, the idea generated considerable interest and controversy. Tesla went immediately to J. P. Morgan, Jr. in search of financing to build a prototype; but Morgan was unconvinced. Tesla also attempted to deal directly with Great Britain's Prime Minister Neville Chamberlain; but when he resigned upon discovering that he had been out-maneuvered by Hitler at Munich, interest in Tesla's new "anti-war weapon technology" eventually collapsed. Nevertheless, by 1937 it was clear that war would soon break out in Europe. Despite being frustrated in his attempts to generate interest and financing for his "peace beam," Tesla sent an elaborate technical paper, including diagrams, to several Allied nations including the United States, Canada, England, France, the Soviet Union, and Yugoslavia, "New Art of Projecting Concentrated Non-Dispersive Energy Through Natural Media." This was the paper that provided the first technical description of what is today called a *charged particle beam weapon*. But what set Tesla's proposal apart from the usual run of fantasy Flash Gordon "death rays" was a unique vacuum chamber with one end open to the atmosphere. Tesla had carefully devised a unique vacuum seal by directing a high-velocity air stream at the tip of his gun to maintain what he considered

---

[26]   Dr. Raymond A. Keller, *Venus Rising: A Concise History of the Second Planet* (Terra Alta, West Virginia: Headline Books, 2015), 125-139, 145, 156.

"high vacua," such as surrounds the launch of a time probe in the Cyther Dome on Venus, as described in the last chapter of *Venus Rising: A Concise History of the Second Planet.*[27] The necessary pumping action, however, was accomplished with the aid of a large Tesla turbine.

While many countries received Tesla's fantastic proposal, the greatest interest came from the Soviet Union. In 1937 the scientist presented a plan to the Amtorg Trading Corporation, an alleged Soviet arms front in New York City; and just two years later, in 1939, one stage of the plan was tested in the USSR and Tesla received a check for $25,000. Tesla hoped that his invention would be used for purely defensive purposes, and thus would become an anti-war machine. Tesla had no qualms about sharing this technology with the Soviet Union insomuch as they were announced foes of Hitler's totalitarian Nazi regime, fearing that Hitler would try and accomplish what other West European tyrants had failed to do- conquer Mother Russia.

Tesla's system required a series of power plants located along a country's coast that would scan the skies in search of enemy aircraft; and since the beam was projected in a straight line, it was only effective for about 200 miles. This figure is very important because it corresponds to the distance of the curvature of the Earth. Tesla also considered peacetime applications for his particle beam, such as the transmission of power without wires over long distances. And yet another radical notion he proposed was to heat up portions of the upper atmosphere to light the sky at night with a man-made aurora borealis.[28] Interestingly, following the collision of a large asteroid body with Venus countless millennia ago, it threw the planet into a retrograde motion and slowed its day from 96 hours to about 243 Earth days. This is the time it takes for Venus to spin around on its axis just once. And because it's so close to the Sun, a year goes by much faster than it does here on Earth. It takes 225 Earth days for Venus to complete one orbit around the Sun; and that means that a day on Venus is a little longer than its year. But since the day and year lengths are similar, one day on Venus is not like a day on Earth. Here, the Sun rises and

---

[27]   Keller, R. A., "Chapter VIII: Gods of Aquarius" (Terra Alta, West Virginia: Headline Books, 2015).

[28]   *Master of Lightning – Nikola Tesla*, section titled "Weapon to End War," broadcast as PBS Documentary in April 2004 (Washington, DC: New Voyage Communications), http://www.pbs.org/tesla/ll/ll_wendwar.html (Accessed 21 November 2016).

sets once each day. However, on Venus the Sun rises every 117 Earth days. This is something that can be very disconcerting to Terrans visiting Venus. It translates into our biological clocks being all thrown out of sync, with the Sun rising two times during each year, even though it is still the same day on Venus. And because Venus rotates backwards, the sun rises in the west and sets in the east.[29] To compensate for this, the surviving Venusians created just such a device to light up their long night sky at sundry intervals. And coupled with the natural bio-florescent life that evolved there, an aurora-like spectacle, often referred to as an "ashen light," graces the dark side of Venus and sometimes can be viewed on the rim of the planet by astronomers at ground-based observatories here on Earth. Because of Tesla's intimate connections with Venus and Venusians, to include his own ancestry, he was probably quite familiar with this device and all its potential applications for peace.

Insofar as the disposition of Nikola Tesla's technical and scientific papers after he died at the height of World War II in 1943, it was natural that the FBI and other U.S. government agencies would be interested in any of his ideas involving advanced technology and their application to weaponry. Some FBI officials were concerned that Tesla's papers might fall into the hands of the Axis powers, or the Soviets; with this latter group being the one that Hoover feared most. And on the morning after the inventor's death, his nephew Sava Kosanovic´ hurried to his uncle's room at the Hotel New Yorker. Sava was an up-and-coming Yugoslav official with suspected connections to the Communist Party in his country. But by the time young Sava arrived, his beloved uncle's body had already been removed. Sava immediately suspected that someone had already gone through his uncle's personal effects insofar as technical papers were missing as well as a black notebook that he knew that Tesla assiduously kept. This was a notebook with several hundred pages, some of which were marked "Government." So, because Adamski was involved with some individuals working with a Tesla-type technology, this would be a matter of deep concern to Director Hoover and the FBI.

In returning to Tesla's case, it was P. E. Foxworth, assistant director of the New York FBI office, who was called in to investigate. According to Foxworth, the government was indeed "vitally interested" in preserving Tesla's papers. Two days after the inventor's death, representatives of the FBI's Office of Alien Property (OAP)

---

[29] Kristen Erickson, "All About Venus," 17 November 2016, *NASA Space Place*, http://spaceplace.nasa.gov/all-about-venus/en/ (Accessed 21 November 2016).

went to his room at the New Yorker Hotel and seized all his possessions. Dr. John G. Trump, an electrical engineer with the National Defense Research Committee of the Office of Scientific Research and Development, was called in to analyze the Tesla papers in OAP custody and following a three-day investigation, Dr. Trump concluded that, "His [Tesla's] thoughts and efforts during at least the past 15 years were primarily of a speculative, philosophical, and somewhat promotional character often concerned with the production and wireless transmission of power; but did not include new, sound, workable principles or methods for realizing such results." Or so they say for public consumption.

Just after World War II, however, there was a renewed interest in beam weapons on the part of the United States government, especially since the Soviets actually paid Tesla for information on the same prior to the outbreak of the global conflagration. It appears that copies of Tesla's papers on particle beam weaponry were sent to Patterson Air Force Base in Dayton, Ohio as part of an operation code-named Project Nick. The research that ensued was heavily funded and placed under the command of Brigadier General L. C. Craigie. Its purpose was to test the feasibility of Tesla's particle beam weapon concept. Details of the experiments were never published. The project was apparently discontinued. However, something very peculiar happened. The copies of Tesla's papers just "disappeared" and nobody knows what happened to them, even to this day. So, when two gentlemen are apparently working on such technology along with George Adamski, this is going to be a special matter of concern for the FBI and many other United States government agencies. That the matter was forwarded to the Cleveland office is also an interesting aside here; for not only did the two men have Ohio addresses, but as reported in Venus Rising,[30] a laboratory of the Radio Corporation of America (RCA) in Cleveland was the purported destination for some of the debris recovered from two crashed flying saucers in New Mexico.

It's an absolute outrage that it took nine years since Tesla's death for his remaining papers and possessions to be released to his dear nephew, Sava Kosanovic, and returned to Belgrade, Yugoslavia, where a museum was created in honor of the great inventor. For many years to follow, under Josip Broz Tito's communist rule, it became extremely difficult for Western journalists and scholars to gain access to the Tesla archive there. And even those who did gain access were only allowed to see

---

[30] Keller, *Venus Rising*, 172

selected papers. This, however, was not the case for Soviet scientists who swarmed there in delegations during the 1950s. Of course, concerns dramatically escalated in 1960 when Soviet Premier Nikita Khrushchev announced to the Supreme Soviet that "a new and fantastic weapon was in the hatching stage." Work on such advanced particle beam weapons also continued in the United States.

In 1958, the Defense Advanced Research Projects Agency (DARPA) began a TOP SECRET project code-named Seesaw. Situated at Lawrence Livermore Laboratory in California, its purpose was to develop a charged-particle beam weapon. And more than ten years and twenty-seven million dollars later, the project was allegedly abandoned "because of the projected high costs associated with implementation as well as the formidable technical problems associated with propagating a beam through very long ranges in the atmosphere." According to the PBS documentary, scientists associated with the project had no knowledge of Tesla's papers. Likely story!

And by the late 1970s, there was fear that the Soviets may have achieved a technological breakthrough. Some American defense analysts concluded that a large charged particle beam weapon facility was under construction near the Sino-Soviet border in southern Russia. The American response to this so-called "technological surprise" was the Strategic Defense Initiative (SDI) announced by President Ronald Reagan in 1983. It became known as the infamous "Star Wars" anti-missile defense shield. Teams of government scientists were urged, "Turn your great talents now to the cause of mankind and world peace, to give us the means of rendering these nuclear weapons impotent and obsolete." The spokesperson in the PBS documentary declared that, "For many years scientists and researchers have sought for Tesla's missing papers with no apparent success. It is conceivable that if Nikola Tesla knew a means for accurately projecting lethal beams of energy through the atmosphere, he may have taken it to the grave with him."[31] But given the circumstances surrounding the confiscation of his papers at the time of the great inventor's death, this seems highly improbable. NASA and Air Force personnel have spoken to me in anonymity, assuring that there is indeed a space program not for public consumption, and that this more advanced agency works with both alien and Tesla technologies.

---

[31] *Master of Lightning – Nikola Tesla*, section titled "Missing Papers," broadcast as PBS Documentary in April 2004 (Washington, DC: New Voyage Communications), http://www.pbs.org/tesla/ll/ll_mispapers.html (Accessed 21 November 2016).

23 March 1953, Office Memorandum from SAC, San Diego (100-8382) to Director, FBI Subject: GEORGE ADAMSKI, was. SECURITY MATTER - C Re San Diego letter to Bureau dated January 28, 1953.

On March 13, 1953 an article in the Riverside "Enterprise" newspaper stated that ADAMSKI in a speech before the Corona, California Lions Club on March 12, 1953, had prefaced his talk on space travel with a statement that "his material had all been cleared with the Federal Bureau of Investigation and Air Force Intelligence." On March 17, 1953 ADAMSKI was contacted at his residence, Palomar Gardens Café, Valley Center, California by agents of the FBI and OSI. ADAMSKI at this time stated that he had not made such a statement. In the presence of the agents he also wrote a letter to the Editor of the Riverside, California "Enterprise" newspaper stating that their article was incorrect and advising them that it was his desire that they correct the statement reading that "his material had all been cleared with the Federal Bureau of Investigation and Air Force Intelligence." The agents observed the mailing of this letter.

ADAMSKI was severely admonished and a signed statement obtained from him that included the following: "I understand that the Federal Bureau of Investigation and the United States Air Force investigate complaints affecting the security of the United States. I understand that they make no recommendations as to the validity or non-validity of these complaints. "I have not and do not intend to make statements to the effect that the U. S. Air Force or Federal Bureau of Investigation have approved material used in my speeches." CLARENCE CARPENTER, (DELETED) California, reporter of the story on ADAMSKI advised the statement, "his material had all been cleared with the Federal Bureau of Investigation and Air Force Intelligence," was a direct quote from his notes. Unless advised contrary by Bureau no further investigation will be conducted.

Analysis: In some manner, Adamski mentioned the interest of the FBI and the Air Force in his UFO research during a lecture to a chapter of the Lions Club. The FBI and Office of Scientific Intelligence (OSI) dispatch agents to Adamski's home and secure a written statement from him attesting to the fact that he will no longer mention that either the FBI or the Air Force has approved the contents of his speeches. In addition, these agents watch him write a letter to the reporter of a California newspaper who covered his Lions Club lecture. In this letter, Adamski informs the reporter that his article was incorrect in declaring that he had made any such statement concerning the approval of the contents of his lecture by any government agency. Both agents observed Adamski mailing this letter to the newspaper office. Adamski was "severely admonished" by these agents. Apparently, various agencies of the government are starting to become concerned about Adamski's activities. They certainly do not wish for Adamski to say anything that reflects the interests of their respective agencies in anything Adamski is saying or doing with respect to UFOs or life on other planets.

10 December 1953, Office Memorandum from SAC, Los Angeles (100-24442) to Director, FBI Subject: GEORGE A. ADAMSKI, aka. SM – C 00: San Diego Re San Diego let to Director 9/22/1952.

On 12/10/53, (DELETED) for the Los Angeles Better Business Bureau, 742 South Hill Street, Los Angeles, California, appeared at the Los Angeles Office and advised (DELETED) that his Bureau is investigating GEORGE ADAMSKI's book, "SAUCERS HAVE LANDED," to determine if it is a fraud. On 12/9/53 ADAMSKI was interviewed by (DELETED) in Los Angeles, at which time ADAMSKI produced a document having a blue seal in the lower left corner, at the top of which appeared three names of Government agents, namely, (DELETED) FBI;" (DELETED) Agent, USAAF;" (DELETED) USAAF." ADAMSKI inferred to (DELETED) that these Government agents had "cleared" him to make speeches concerning flying saucers. COLSTON stated that he did not pay too much attention to the document, but that the seal looked "faked." (DELETED) advised that his Bureau intends to label ADAMSKI's book a fraud since there seems to be absolutely no basis for some of his claims. He indicated that his book has sold over 100,000 copies and ADAMSKI is getting a great deal of publicity by appearing on radio programs and by making lectures on the subject of flying saucers. ADAMSKI claims to have taken a trip around the moon in an interplanetary ship piloted by men from Venus. ADAMSKI, according to (DELETED) returned to his home near San Diego on 12/9/53. The above information is being furnished to the Bureau and the San Diego Office for whatever action deemed appropriate. OSI, Los Angeles, has been advised. REG. AIR MAIL CEW: VMD Cc: 2 – San Diego (100-8382) (REG.)

Analysis: A representative of the Los Angeles, California, Better Business Bureau suspects that Adamski may be perpetuating a fraud with his book, Flying Saucers Have Landed, and so informs the local FBI office. The popularity of Adamski's book and attendant lectures is attracting the attention of agents beyond the immediate jurisdiction of the San Diego office. Contrary to his statement to the agents who previously visited his home, Adamski is now not only stating that some government agencies approve the contents of his talks on flying saucers, but is producing signed documents testifying to that effect.

16 December 1953, Office Memorandum from L. B. Nichols to Mr. Tolson[32] Subject: GEORGE A. ADAMSKI SECURITY MATTER – C COAUTHOR OF "FLYING SAUCERS HAVE LANDED" SYNOPSIS:

George A. Adamski, 62, described as mentally unbalanced and a "crackpot" of Palomar Gardens, Valley Center, California, is coauthor with one Desmond Leslie of the book "Flying Saucers Have Landed," first printed in September, 1953, and now in its fifth printing. Adamski claims to have taken trip around Moon in an interplanetary ship piloted by men from Venus. A 3-13-53 article in the Riverside, California, "Enterprise" states Adamski, in a speech on space travel before the Corona, California, Lions Club 3-12-53, stated his material had all been cleared with FBI and Air Force Intelligence.

On 3-17-53, Adamski interviewed by SA(DELETED)[33] San Diego Office, (DELETED) and (DELETED) Office of Special Investigations agents. Adamski denied making statement, wrote letter to the editor correcting record and gave signed statement witnessed by the three Agents to effect he had not and did not

---

[32]   John Stuart Cox and Theoharis, Athan G., The Boss: J. Edgar Hoover and the Great American Inquisition. (Philadelphia, Pennsylvania: Temple University Press, 1988), 108. Since the 1940s, rumors circulated that Hoover was homo sexual. Historians John Stuart Cox and Athan G. Theoharis speculated that Clyde Tolson, whom Hoover elevated to the position of an associate director of the FBI as well as his primary heir, may have also been his lover. Allegedly, Hoover hunted down and threatened anyone who made insinuations about his sexuality.

[33]   SA indicates that a special agent was assigned to the case, interviewing Adamski.

intend to make statements that the FBI and OSI approved his material. He said he understood these agencies make no recommendations.

Copy of statement demanded by and given to Adamski 3-17-53. By letter dated 12-11-53, to Director from (DELETED) Better Business Bureau, Los Angeles, California (DELETED) states Adamski exhibited a document signed by three Agents purporting to clear his material. (DELETED) on 12-10-53, advised Los Angeles Office the Better Business Bureau intends to label Adamski's book as a fraud. Air Force officers in Pentagon likewise received letter from (DELETED) dated 12-11-53 SAC (DELETED) at San Diego instructed (INSERTS HERE "by telephone on 12-14-53") to have Agent, accompanied by OSI, read riot act to Adamski in no uncertain terms, diplomatically retrieve copy of signed statement, if possible, admonish him for statements and false representations. (DELETED AND THEN INSERTS HERE "to advise as to results.") Proposed letter to Better Business Bureau prepared.

RECOMMENDATION: That the attached letter to Mr. (DELETED) Research Division, Better Business Bureau, Los Angeles, California, be forwarded pointing out true facts of the FBI's relationship with Adamski and fact this Bureau has not endorsed, approved or cleared Adamski's speeches or book.

Attachment cc - Mr. Ladd cc - Mr. Belmont cc - Mr. Jones REW: ps

Memorandum to Mr. Tolson, December 16, 1953 (PAGE TWO)

DETAILS: Bureau file 100-395273 reflects that George Adamski, age 62, born April 17, 1891 in Poland, according to (DELETED) is a "crackpot." Individuals in the community regard him as "mentally unbalanced" in that he claims to have taken a trip around the Moon in an interplanetary ship piloted by men from Venus. He currently resides at the place of his employment, Palomar Gardens Café, Valley Center, California. He entered the United States in 1893 through the port of New York; served from 1913-16 in the United States Army; worked as a painter in Yellowstone National Park in 1916, in the flour mills in Portland, Oregon, in 1918, in the concrete business in California in 1921, and in 1926 began lecturing on philosophy. He never received a college degree; his title of professor is a nickname; he is married but has no children. We have never investigated Adamski.

George Adamski, together with one Desmond Leslie, co-authored a book selling for $3.50 known as "Flying Saucers Have Landed." First printed in September

1953, and copyrighted 1953 by "The British Book Center, Incorporated," 420 West 45th Street, New York, New York, the book, in December 1953, is in its fifth printing. Adamski claims he has sold more than 100,000 copies of this 232-page book. In it he sets forth photographs purported to be of flying saucers in flight and on the ground. Also included are "writings from another planet" which Adamski claims came into his possession after he took a photograph of a flying saucer and "a little man" from the spaceship took the photographic plate from him and some days later returned a photographic plate to him on the California desert which, when developed, disclosed "writings from another planet."

On 12-10-53, (DELETED) Research Division of the Better Business Bureau, 1010 Lincoln Building, 742 South Hill Street, Los Angeles, California, came to the Los Angeles Office in person and stated the Better Business Bureau is investigating Adamski's book, "Flying Saucers Have Landed," with a view to branding it a fraud. (DELETED) said in connection therewith he had, on 12-9-53, interviewed Adamski who produced a document having a blue seal in the lower left corner and at the top appeared three names of government agents: (DELETED) FBI; (DELETED) Agent, USAAF, and (DELETED) Agent, USAAF. According to (DELETED) it was inferred by Adamski the above-named government agents have "cleared" Adamski to make speeches concerning flying saucers. (DELETED) said he did not pay too much attention to the document, but that it looked faked.

By letter dated December 11, 1953, the above-named (DELETED) advised the Director of substantially the same information as related by (DELETED) to the Los Angeles Office 12-10-53. (DELETED) stated the Better Business Bureau was interested in whether or not the document, in possession of Adamski, is authentic and whether the FBI endorsed the "Professor's" book. *The Director inquired, "What about this?"*

As of the end of 1953, FBI Director J. Edgar Hoover took an active interest in the George Adamski case. Photo source: www.express.co.uk.

THE UTOPIAN THREAT

The increasing flurry of memoranda between an expanding number of FBI field offices, coupled with the unprecedented international popularity of Adamski and Leslie's Flying Saucers Have Landed, at last caught the attention of the FBI Director J. Edgar Hoover. While he would not publish his anti-communist book, *Masters of Deceit*,[34] until 1958, it was apparent at the start of the Cold War that Americans were decidedly opposed to communist expansion anywhere in the world and felt that it was the duty of the United States to both stem and push it back, wherever and whenever it raised its ugly head. Hoover's opposition to communism extended back to the First Red Scare that took place immediately following World War I, however; so, it seems logical enough to assume that he must have been seeing "red flags" all over Adamski's and the other contactees' accounts of meetings with extra-

---

[34] J. Edgar Hoover, *Masters of Deceit* (New York, New York: Pocket Books, 1958).

terrestrials hailing from some "utopian" society that had evolved on Venus and other nearby planets in the solar system.

Hoover was born on 1 January 1895 in Washington, D.C., the son of Anna Marie (née Scheitlin; 1860–1938), who was of German Swiss descent, and Dickerson Naylor Hoover, Sr. (1856–1921), who was of English and German ancestry. For most of his life, Hoover lived in the Washington, D.C., area. Politically, he followed a conservative line of thinking. He attended Central High School in the nation's capital and was an active member of its Officers' Training Corps program, where he participated on the debate team, arguing against women getting the right to vote and against the abolition of the death penalty. One would rightly suppose that Hoover would end up being so reactionary insofar as both of his parents were so authoritarian and stern in raising him. But much to his credit, the young Hoover remained focused in his studies, and went on to obtain a Bachelor of Laws degree from the George Washington University Law School in 1916 and a Master of Laws degree in the following year from the same university. While the young man was studying law, he worked as a messenger in the Orders Department of the Library of Congress; and during this time, Hoover took for his mentor the United States Postal Inspector Anthony Comstock of New York City, who waged a relentless battle against fraud, vice, pornography, and birth control.

But it was right after graduating with his master's degree that the industrious Hoover was hired by the Justice Department to work in the War Emergency Division, where it didn't take long before he became the head of that division's Alien Enemy Bureau, authorized by President Wilson at the beginning of World War I to arrest and jail disloyal foreigners without the benefit of trial. Hoover received yet additional government authority from the Congress' passing of the 1917 Espionage Act. Since Hoover was of German descent and fluent in the German language, he was put to work immediately in that section of the new bureau dealing with German and German-American activities taking place in the United States. We must keep in mind that many German Americans and European immigrants were coming under suspicion at this time because the new Soviet government in Russia, headed by Lenin, had pulled out of the Allied command in fighting the Germans. Therefore, out of a list of 1,400 suspicious Germans living in the U.S., the Bureau arrested 98 and designated 1,172 as being subject to arrest.

In any event, in just two years, Hoover became head of the Bureau of Investigation's new General Intelligence Division. This was also known as the

Radical Division because its goal was to monitor and disrupt the work of domestic radicals. Thus, emerged America's First Red Scare, wherein Hoover was taking a key role in carrying out the now-regarded as infamous "Palmer Raids." In these actions, Hoover helped in rounding up, arresting and deporting alleged anarchists and leftist radicals throughout 1919 and 1920.[35] This is why Adamski must have been seen as a special interest individual to Hoover, for the contactee was a character aptly fitting the profile of a suspected radical back in these early days of the FBI Director's career, especially with his Polish background and occasional "anti-American" comments made in the Palomar Gardens Café or on the flying saucer lecture circuit. During the early years of hunting radicals, Hoover chose as his able assistant, George Ruch. Together, they began monitoring a variety of radicals with the intent to punish, arrest, or deport those whose politics they decided were dangerous. Some of the more notable immigrant targets during this period were the Pan-African nationalist Marcus Garvey, the socialist and feminist leader Rose Pastor Stokes, the Caribbean communist Cyril V. Briggs, anarchists Emma Goldman and Alexander Berkman, as well as the future Supreme Court justice Felix Frankfurter. Of the latter, Hoover maintained that Frankfurther was "the most dangerous man in the United States," most likely because he was one of the founders of he American Civil Liberties Union, in addition to serving as an architect for so many of President Franklin D. Roosevelt's progressive New Deal programs.[36] Overall, that Hoover would one day decide to focus his attention on the likes of George Adamski indicates that the xeno-phobic director really put the contactee in with some good company in American history.

Hoover's star rapidly ascended in the Bureau of Investigation. By 1921, Hoover was promoted to deputy head and, in 1924 the Attorney General made him the acting director. And on 10 May 1924, President Calvin Coolidge appointed Hoover as the sixth Director of the Bureau of Investigation. Some historians believe this action was taken partly in response to allegations that the prior director, William J. Burns, was involved in the Teapot Dome scandal. In any event, at the time of Hoover's assumption of the director's duties, the Bureau had approximately 650

---

[35]   Curt Gentry, *J. Edgar Hoover: The Man and the Secrets* (New York, New York: W. W. Norton and Company, 2001).

[36]   Anthony Summers, "The secret life of J. Edgar Hoover," 31 December 2011, *Observer*, London, United Kingdom.

employees, including 441 Special Agents, compared to the 35,000 working with the organization today.[37]

Keep in mind that even before Adamski was writing about his contacts with Venusians, he enjoyed some notoriety as an author of science fiction. And this was an area where its fans, writers and publishers were frequently scrutinized by the FBI as possible instigators of subversion. In the vast universe of science fiction, there have always been two notable strains. First, there is the New Fandom faction. This group was rather innocuous, at least insofar as it was only reading science fiction for its pure entertainment value. On the other hand, there were the Futurians. This faction was highly politicized, so much so, that its adherents were attempting to implement the utopian principles of societal organization introduced in the pages of science fiction magazines directly into the American body politic.

Among the ranks of the Futurians could be found a young Isaac Asimov, an immigrant from the Soviet Union, prominent biochemist and aspiring writer of both popular science and science fiction. In 1939, we find Asimov enroute from his home in California to attend both the World's Fair and the first World Science Fiction Convention. Asimov must have felt that he had died and went to heaven.

The search for extraterrestrial intelligence (SETI) may represent a modern gnosis in the making. How will SETI and UFO disclosures impact the evolution of society and its structures? These are questions considered by Isaac Asimov, the writer of popular science and science fiction books. Book above first published in 1979 by Ballantine, New York.

---

[37] "Frequently Asked Questions," undated, United States Department of Justice, https://www.fbi.gov/about/faqs (Accessed 20 October 2016).

At the World's Fair, he was one of the select Americans to get a sneak peek at such new marvels as 3-D movies (that are all so now the rage), fax machines, fluorescent lighting, FM radio, Lucite, nylon, television and much more. All of this had to do with the fair's theme of "Building the World of Tomorrow." And at the science fiction convention, the young Asimov continued to imbibe in inspiring, utopian dreams of exploring distant planets and learning about all sorts of exotic new life forms and extraterrestrial civilizations, and lest one forget, alternative ways of organizing our own. Such heady days these must have been!

From such marvelous experiences, Asimov came to believe that, "science fiction should rise to a vision of a greater world, a greater future for the whole of mankind, and should utilize idealistic convictions for aid in a generally cooperative and diverse movement for the betterment of the world along democratic, impersonal and unselfish lines." Naturally, Hoover was aware of this utopian and leftist trend, as many of the Futurians were involved in suspicious causes like the promotion of atheism, humanism and yes, even communism. The FBI director was also cognizant of the fact that some of the Futurians were members of the American Communist Party and hence they were to be considered as "dangerously red."[38]

Adamski's earlier entry into the realm of science fiction clearly placed him in the Futurians' camp; and therefore, it is not entirely unreasonable to assume that Adamski might have been under FBI surveillance from an earlier time, preceding his involvement in the flying saucer movement.

CONTINUING FBI SURVEILLANCE OF ADAMSKI

With Hoover now taking a personal interest in the Adamski case, the San Diego office issues an office memorandum to the Director, FBI, on 15 December 1953, subject GEORGE A. ADAMSKI, aka Professor ADAMSKI, George A. ADAMSKI, George A. Adamsky, with a security classification of "C," presumably meaning that the document was confidential. This memorandum was written in regards to the Los Angeles letter to the Bureau, dated 10 December 1953, the San Diego letter to the Bureau, dated 22 September 1953, and telephone calls from the Bureau (J.

---

[38] George Pendle, *Strange Angel: Otherworldly Life of Rocket Scientist John Whiteside Parsons* (Orlando, Florida: Har court, Inc., 2005), 154, 156.

Edgar Hoover) to San Diego on 14 and 15 December 1953. Clearly, the Director was becoming impatient and needed the rundown on this Adamski character. Of course, the San Diego letter to the Bureau on 22 September advised that no additional investigation was being conducted with respect to this case; but for the information of the Bureau and the Los Angeles office of the FBI, it was reported that Adamski owned and operated the Palomar Gardens Café, located about five miles east of Rincon, California, at a point where the highway branches off leading to the Mt. Palomar Observatory. At that time, Palomar was considered the most powerful telescope and astronomical facility in the world. When any Department of Defense[39] officials became concerned about the appearance of some new astronomical phenomenon, Palomar Observatory is the place they would automatically turn to in the hopes of obtaining better resolution photographs of the anomaly.

Naturally, it became a matter of concern to the FBI and other intelligence agencies that a Polish immigrant who occasionally made critical statements of the Air Force and other government agencies, was living right next door to this important facility. Of Adamski, the San Diego office informs the Director that, "He is an amateur astronomer and for the past several years this office has received complaints relative to the subject's having seen flying saucers in the vicinity of his establishment. He exhibits photographs purported to be of flying saucers to patrons of his establishment. OSI of the Air Force has done considerable investigation relative to these complaints and lends no credence to the truthfulness of ADAMSKI's statements." In addition, the Director's attention was invited to the San Diego office's letters dated 28 January 1953 and 23 March 1953, both regarding the activities of George Adamski. The following statement, obtained and signed by Adamski on 17 March 1953, was also forwarded to the Director and the Los Angeles office along with the 15 December memorandum:

---

[39] On 18 September 1947, just months after the Roswell crash, the Department of War was officially renamed the Department of Defense. Were we sending a message to the extraterrestrials that we would not be the first to take aggressive action against their spacecraft, but would defend ourselves if attacked, or perhaps just provoked?

Palomar Gardens
March 17, 1953
To Whom It May Concern:

I, George Adamski, hereby make the following signed statement to (DELETED) Agent, F.B.I., and (DELETED) and (DELETED), Agents of the Air Force. This statement is voluntary and no threats or promises have been made to me. I understand that the Federal Bureau of Investigation and the United States Air Force investigate complaints affecting the security of the United States. I understand that they make no recommendations as to the validity or non-validity of these complaints. I have not and do not intend to make statements to the effect that the U. S. Air Force or Federal Bureau of Investigation have approved material used in my speeches. I have read the above statement and it is true and correct to the best of my knowledge. Signed, /s/ GEO_ ADAMSKI

George Adamski
Star Route Valley Center, California
GA:lm

The statement was witnessed and signed by one agent of the FBI and two special agents of the Inspector General, Office of Scientific Investigation, U. S. Air Force. Copies of this statement were sent by COL:CS via registered airmail to both the Director and the Los Angeles office (100-24442) with high priority. The memorandum also avows that per the Director's instructions, "ADAMSKI will be contacted in the immediate future, at which time he will be requested to cease and desist making any reference to the FBI in his talks or in any publications which he might issue."

Naturally, the Director was informed that he would be advised directly concerning the results of this contact. Toward the end of the following year, the Detroit, Michigan, office of the FBI had been drawn into the ongoing Adamski investigation. In an office memorandum to the Director from the SAC, Detroit (65-2677), dated 30 November 1954, reference was made to a letter from J. Edgar Hoover dated 8 October 1954 regarding the Detroit Flying Saucer Club and its activities.

The subject of the memorandum was "DETROIT FLYING SAUCER CLUB, ES PIONAGE – X." Perhaps this is where the real "X Files" began. The author of the Detroit FBI memorandum writes that, "The purpose of this letter is to set out for the information of the Bureau, the activities of the Detroit Flying Saucer Club, as they are known. This is done chronologically.

"On May 18, 1954, (DELETED) advised that she had been attending meetings concerning flying saucers, rockets to the Moon, etc., which she felt could be subversive. On May 27, 1954, (DELETED) and (DELETED) talked in Detroit on flying saucers. They were alarmed at the nature of the remarks; such as 'We are Americans, but....' and that we should reduce our arms and would blow ourselves up with the H-Bomb, because visitors from outer space were afraid that we had started something that would get out of hand. Another lecturer in Detroit, was TRUMAN BETHURUM. The sponsors of these speakers were HELEN REEVE, LAURA MARXER, HENRY MADAY and RONALD COOK. According to pamphlets furnished by (DELETED), a "Flying Saucer Review Group" was to be formed. This was headed by HENRY MADAY, 364 W. Lewiston, Ferndale, Michigan, who uses the pen name, JARED LYON. He is editor, Bresser Cross Index Directory, Detroit. They advised that LAURA MARXER was the Station WWJ-TV personality "MIDGE" in the "Playschool" program.

"On July 13, 1954, (DELETED) advised that MADAY was bringing to Detroit, someone who talked to people from Venus, Clarion, etc., who are more highly advanced than Earth people. They advocated the Golden Rule as the only workable rule. A meeting was to be held on July 15, 1954. (DELETED) also furnishes a letter from one (DELETED) encouraging him in his interest in flying saucers. (DELETED) felt such an organization could use the flying saucer scare as political propaganda or form a pseudo-religious view. He said they opposed the atomic bomb and warfare.

"(DELETED) advised she attended the July 15, 1954 meeting of the flying saucer group. The purpose was to organize a flying saucer club in Detroit. HENRY MADAY was behind it. (DELETED SENTENCE HERE) An organizational letter was passed out at this meeting stat ing the purpose of the 'Flying Saucer Club of Detroit' was:

1.   ***Exchange ideas, and in general, become aware of the flying saucer picture.***

> 2. *Invite national "saucer" speakers to Detroit, and enlighten the public.*
>
> 3. *Spread information on flying saucers.*
>
> 4. *To engage in those aspects of 'saucer' interests, especially appealing to each member, such as, astronomy, engineering, spiritual, curiosity, etc.*

"The temporary committee setting forth these aims were: HENRY MADAY, LAURA MARXER, BRYANT REEVE, N. D. HUNTER, HOWARD KEHL, HELEN REEVE, and JOHN HOFFMAN. At this July 15, 1954, meeting, GEORGE ADAMSKI introduced CLAR ENCE A. TROUT, of E. Outer Drive, Detroit, who reported seeing a flying saucer July 14, 1954, at 10:30 p.m.

"(DELETED) advised that the first official meeting of the Detroit Flying Saucer Club (DFSC) would be held August 19, 1954. "The Detroit Times of 20 August 1954, in an article on the August 19, 1954 meeting, said that 'Scientists were wrong is discounting the flying saucer theory' and that the Club would act as a clearing house for local sightings, and submit reports to the Army test center, Wright Patterson Air Force Base, Dayton.

"(DELETED) advised that the August 19, 1954 meeting consisted mostly of people saying they had seen saucers. Mr. REEVES, an engineer, commented on each reported sighting. JOHN HOFFMAN, an advertising man, and a Mr. TROUT, of Continental Motors, reported sightings. "(DELETED), Farmington, Michigan, advised on September 29, 1954, that the officers of the DFSC, 6432 Cass Avenue, Detroit, were: HENRY MADAY, President; LAURA MARX ER, Vice-President; DOLORES M. COYNE, Secretary; and JOHN C. HOFFMAN, Treasurer. "He said the club was going to petition the President of the United States to make public all government information on flying saucers. He also stated that by letter, September 25, 1954, LAURA MARXER advised him he was a group leader in the club, and his duties would be to keep up with the latest developments and advise his group, the names of which he would receive from Miss COYNE.

"The Detroit Free Press of September 29, 1954, said in an article that the DFSC met September 28, 1954, and DESMOND LESLIE, British flying saucer authority, spoke, stating that GEORGE ADAMSKI made contact two years ago with space people in a California desert.

"(DELETED) a letter September 30, 1954, from DOLORES M. COYNE, Secretary, DFSC, setting out the discussion group in the Farmington area as: Mr.

and Mrs. BAILEY, 32740 Northwestern Highway, Detroit. ALFRED S. STUDER, 28993 Parkhill, Detroit. M. K. ZIMMER, 29581 Belfast, Detroit.

"(DELETED) received a letter from her October 4, 1954, adding to the above list: Miss LUCY RAMBO, 30203 Overdale Ct., Rte. 4, Farmington. (PARAGRAPH DELETED HERE).

"He advised the object of group discussions, according to MARXER, was:

1. *To indoctrinate people to receive space people.*
2. *Mass landings in Detroit in October (not further explained).*
3. *A saucer landed at 4:30 a.m., September 30, 1954, at Rotunda Drive and Southfield (Detroit) with strange greenish men in brown uniforms.*
4. *Beginning in the 1950s, George Adamski and Desmond Leslie's Flying Saucers Have Landed inspired many to join local UFO clubs.*

Unseen psychic forces (no further explanation). (PARAGRAPH DELETED HERE).[40]

"(DELETED) BAILEY said she was an atheist. The main discussion was about religion, science, and double talk, (DELETED) said. Twenty such discussion groups exist. MARXER said there would be landings in Detroit in October, but she could be wrong. (SENTENCE DELETED HERE).

"(DELETED) said a group leaders' meeting was held November 6, 1954, at Ed. SANDERS, 7323 Mayburn, Dearborn, Michigan. Seventeen were there. He did not consider any of it subversive. The Board of Directors of the DFSC are: HENRY MADAY, President; LAURA MARXER, Vice-President; DOLORES M. COYNE, Secretary; JOHN C. HOFFMAN, Treasurer, HOWARD KEHL, RANDALL COC and MADELINE MENDE, Directors.

---

[40] These deletions give credence to the FBI's interest in UFOs as a phenomenon linked to spiritualism and the occult. This is not surprising in lieu of Jack Parsons, founder of the Jet Propulsion Laboratory (JPL) in Pasadena, California, and other scientists attached to Defense Department's weapons development programs, manifesting a fascination and even participation in these arcane topics during their off-duty time.

"(DELETED) said the purpose of this leaders' meeting was to discuss how to handle issues arising in group meetings. These were: Religious Group representation to the Board of Directors of the club.

"The group leaders are supposed to control discussion, and not offend any religious belief."

Beginning in the 1950s, George Adamski and Desmond Leslie's *Flying Saucers Have Landed* inspired many to join local UFO clubs. Little did anyone realize that their daily activities were being scrutinized by the FBI Counterintelligence Program (COINTELPRO). *See http://www. roystoncartoons.com/2010/03/ufo-cartoons-watch-skies.html.*

Of course, this is directly in line with the Objects of the Theosophical Society. Given the backgrounds of Adamski and Leslie, this should come as no surprise. But it wasn't religious concerns that mostly worried the attendees at these early flying saucer meetings, but the fear of communist infiltration. In the next paragraph of the Detroit FBI office memorandum, it goes on to state that, "At this Michigan meeting, FRANK R. SCHUSTER, a group leader, 3022 Chalmers, Detroit, said that JOHN HOFFMAN opposed group meetings because of accusations against them of subversive activities. An unidentified person said he did not think it true, but it was alleged one member of the Board of Directors was a Communist. MADAY answered this by saying he would mention no names, but the accuser should see him about this, and the accused was not a Communist. He said fellow travelers could get in or infiltrate the club, but he was at a loss as to any way of controlling that. As a result of this meeting, (DELETED) felt the group was either subversive, or a new religious group. He felt it all stems from ADAMSKI in California. He said one RIC WILKINSON, a flying saucer speaker, had moved to Detroit."

The general climate of fear and paranoia, so prevalent during the early 1950s, was creeping into the group and destroying its cohesion. The memorandum continues, "At this meeting, MADAY said that had saucer landings occurred in Detroit, in October, the group leaders would have been first to know it. He said he reported to ADAMSKI the predictions of MARXER, and ADAMSKI felt she should not predict more than 30 days in advance, and, even that was no good sometimes."

What is interesting here is that Maday, as president of the club, is reporting directly to George Adamski. Considering member Schuster's concerns expressed above, about the controversy stemming from Adamski out in California, this type of action demonstrated little political autonomy or managerial authority for the DFSC. Adamski's concerns about prophecies seems justified, too, considering the higher standards by which religious organizations are judged vs. secular ones, that are mostly dealing with scientific investigations on an objective basis. It makes sense that the leader of the contactee movement would like to keep it steered in this direction, rather than getting bogged down in endless theological debates. At this juncture, an entire paragraph is deleted.

Then the memorandum continues as follows: "(DELETED) LAURA MARXER (DELETED) was resigning from the Board of Directors of the Club (DELETED) she was going to show the film, 'The Day the Earth Stood Still,' around Michigan, as a result of having met two men (not named). She said ADAMSKI, in California, was her God, even admitting his earthly faults." One can only begin to imagine what Director Hoover thought of this report about Adamski being seen as God to Laura Marxer. Hoover probably wondered how many other people perceived Adamski in the same way. No, this was not going to be a file that would be quickly closed, put out of sight and out of mind. Perhaps this Adamski character, for all his rhetoric about utopian Venus, was a dangerous, communist infiltrator. He would continue to be the focus of attention and scrutiny by special agents of the FBI dispatched by the orders of Director Hoover. The identity of the two men who met with Marxer and urged her to show the movie, *Day the Earth Stood Still*, even into the twenty-first century remains a mystery; but they may very well have been Venusians, or at least individuals claiming to be Venusians and occasionally seen in the company of George Adamski.

Hakan Blomqvist, the leading authority on the contactee phenomenon in Europe, declared that in his personal investigations of many experiencer cases in his home country of Sweden, he has discovered independent witness confirmation that the contactee did meet up with some type of "strangers," regardless of who they might have been. The intrepid Swedish investigator wrote, "We find this also in the Adamski case. Lou Zinsstag mentions that when Adamski stayed in a hotel in Basel in 1959 he was now and then visited by his contacts. Lou decided to check on this and asked the hotel manager and the porter. Both men answered, 'There are several men who come at nine o'clock, but never more than two at a time.'"[41]

The comings and goings of mysterious individuals in visiting contactees along the routes of their tours in bars or hotel/motel rooms either before or after their public presentations has been well established. But those skeptical of Adamski have long asserted that these special visitors were not Venusians or even agents of some TOP SECRET government agency. Rather, they have generated derogatory speculation that Adamski was having secret homosexual trysts, joining in threesomes.[42]

---

[41] Hakan Blomqvist, "Marc Hallet – A Critical Appraisal of George Adamski," 30 July 2015, Hakan Blomqvist's blog, http://ufoarchives.blogspot.com/2015/07/marc-hallet-critical-appraisal-of.html (Accessed 27 October 2016).

[42] Marc Hallet and Richard W. Heiden, *A Critical Appraisal of George Adamski, the Man Who Spoke to the Space Brothers* (2015), https://archive.org/stream/ACriticalAppraisalOfGeorgeAdamskiTheManWhoSpokeToTheSpace Brothers/A%20 Critical%20Appraisal%20of%20George%20Adamski%20-%20The%20Man%20 Who%20Spoke% 20to%20the%20Space%20Brothers_djvu.txt (Accessed 27 October 2016), excerpt from page 184: "During Adamski's trips alone to Los Angeles, or during his trips elsewhere in the world, he always needed to stay at hotels, because, he claimed, if space people wanted to contact him suddenly, it was the best place for it to happen without attracting attention. In Europe, his co-workers noticed that he received visits from young men in his room. Adamski said that they were space brothers. But according to what he had said about the space brothers on other occasions, the latter seemed to be older — about thirty or forty years old, such as those he pointed out at restaurant tables or in a crowd, saying they were space people. Here again, one can only make

However, for Blomqvist, this seems doubtful. The Swedish ufolgist states that, "To my knowledge, there are no facts supporting such a hypothesis."[43] In any case, this was the type of musing that would have caught the avid attention of Hoover, so we can be sure that Adamski was probably being tailed by orders from the Director over the course of his entire life.

All the members of the DFSC became subjects of intense interest for Hoover. The memorandum's author continues, reporting to the Director that, "(DELETED) furnished this office on November 18, 1954, some literature put out by Dr. CHARLES LAUGHEAD, 407 Clarendon Road, East Lansing, Michigan, which (DELETED) obtained at a flying saucer discussion or class. LAUGHEAD's material is in the form of a letter, with attachments to American editors and publishers, stating that he feels they should publish it. He claims messages are received by extra sensory perception from other planets, which are watching the earth. He said one Mrs. DOROTHY MARTIN, Oak Park, Illinois, receives the messages, mostly as lessons for flying saucer clubs.[44] He said she one day picked up her pencil, and it began to write for her in the form of these messages (apparently, it has been writing ever since). LAUGHEAD's letters to editors are dated August 30, 1954 and September 17, 1954. One dated April 24, 1954, captioned 'Telepathy Our Common Means of Communication Dr. SEARLE BEIGLOW of Lansing, Michigan.' It says he was a physician and psychiatrist who suffered much, and was persecuted for his unorthodox lessons in mental disease. He seems to be the contact with outer space."

The connection of flying saucer reports with enhanced psychic abilities in the UFO experiencers may have also been an area that sparked some interest on Hoover's part. As we now know, both United States and Soviet spooks studied paranormal powers in certain individuals in order to obtain a Cold War advantage. One of the United States government organizations working on these types of special

---

suppositions, knowing that some old heterosexual males become sexually attracted to boys or young men when their sexual potential decreases. One thing is sure: when Ray Stanford knew Adamski, he and his friends were teenage boys, but Adamski never had an inappropriate attitude towards them."

[43] *Op cit*

[44] For a complete biography of Dorothy Martin, a.k.a. "Sister Thedra," please see Fred Saluga (author) and Raymond Keller (contributing editor), *West Virginia: Paranormal Gateway* (Terra Alta, West Virginia: Headline Books, 2023),22-62.

projects throughout this critical time was the Defense Advanced Research Projects Agency (DARPA). Even back in the day, DARPA was well known for pushing the boundaries of science and technology in search of ways to give Uncle Sam a decided military edge over the Soviet Bear. DARPA technicians were constantly coming up with new devices that could be deployed in the service of Cold War spies and warriors: robotic pack animals, self-navigating vehicles, plant-based jet fuel, etc. But a lesser-known Cold War-era project in DARPA's "bag of magic tricks" was its investigation into how paranormal phenomena like extrasensory perception (ESP) might be used by the United States to secure an advantage over the former Soviet Union on numerous fronts. And of equal importance, United States intelligence operatives from the highest echelons needed to find out what the Soviets were accomplishing along avenues of similar investigation to employ against us and other nations in the so-called "free world." It has now become clear that DARPA was working closely in its psychic investigations with the Washington, D.C., think tank, the Research and Development Corporation (RAND). DARPA and RAND investigators determined that paranormal research by the Soviets was primarily focused on physical science, engineering and quantifiable results.

On the other hand, in the United States, counterpart investigators tended to be psychologists endeavoring to explore the human mind. The bottom line of all of this, as reported in the 1973 DARPA commissioned study entitled Paranormal Phenomena, was that "the U.S. has failed to significantly advance our understanding of paranormal phenomena." The astute authors of this joint report were concerned, however, that the Soviets might win the race to harness the forces of the supernatural to their own advantage much as they had threatened to win the space race decades earlier when they launched the Sputnik satellite.

"If paranormal phenomena exist," concluded RAND analysts P. T. Van Dyke and Mario L. Juncosa, "the thrust of Soviet research appears more likely to lead to explanation, control and application than [does] U.S. research." The intelligence analysts cited above both acknowledge that the joint study was limited, largely because it was based on a small sampling of works available at the time. But among this sampling could be found a decade of abstracts from the parapsychology section of *Psychological Abstracts*, a print version of the PsycINFO abstract database of psychological literature. What these "somewhat impressionistic" abstracts revealed about Soviet efforts, they admitted, could not always be considered with any high degree of reliability insofar as they were mostly centered on "frequently imprecise reports of Western visitors to the Soviet Union."

Just what J. Edgar Hoover knew about the true extent of Soviet parapsychological research in the mid-1950s, at the height of the Cold War, is not known. But insofar as Hoover's concern about Soviet spy activities in the United States, it only seems logical that he would keep himself informed by his agents in the field of any new techniques the Soviets might be employing to penetrate our extant national security measures. At least so far as telepathy is concerned, Soviet research dates from the early 1920s when a program was established at the Institute for Brain Research at Leningrad State University. The Soviets were fascinated with telepathy, which their investigators referred to as a type of "biological communication." Military strategists in the Soviet Union also saw some possibilities in using telepathy as a "ship-to-shore way of communicating with submarines without using electronic equipment." Additionally, they considered training their cosmonauts to develop and use precognitive abilities to "foresee and to avoid accidents in space."

ORGANIZATION OF SOVIET ACTIVITY

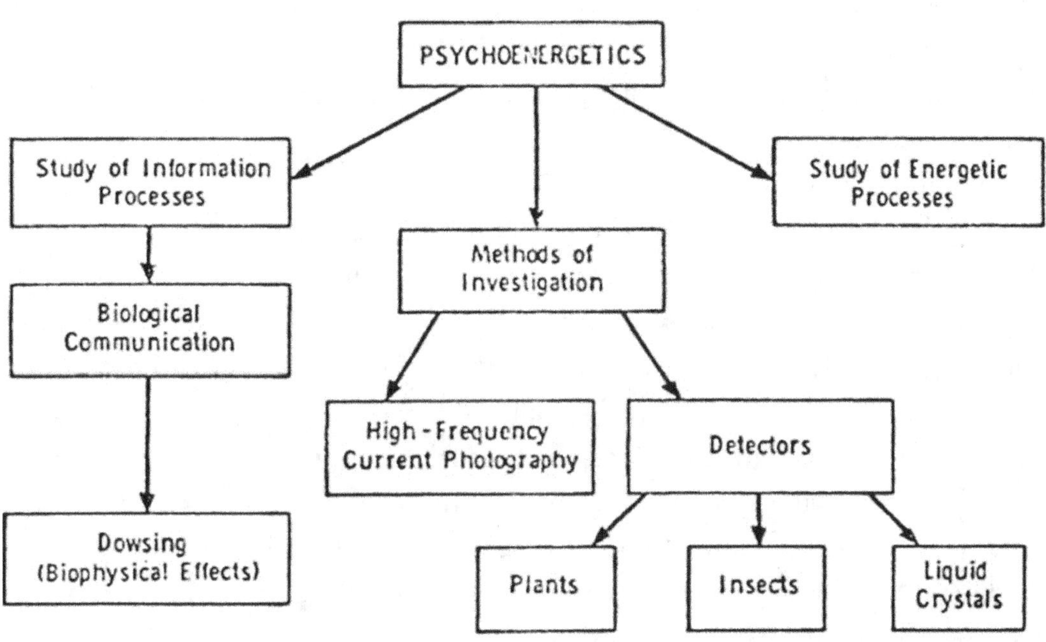

For Soviet military planners, telepathy could be utilized as a type of biological communication to avoid intercept of their radio transmissions. See https://blogs. scientificamerican.com/news-blog/us-and-soviet-spooks studied-parano-2008-10-29/.

It seems that the Soviets were also interested in exploring the possibilities of utilizing psychokinesis in furthering their espionage activities. Intelligence strategists pondered the use of mental imagery to move objects as a way of literally "disrupting the electrical systems associated with an ICBM's (intercontinental ballistic missile) guidance program." The Soviets appeared to be more inclined than American scientists in seriously considering that paranormal phenomena might be some sort of product of the "bioenergetics," or the energy given off by the metabolic processes of living things.

According to this theory, all people exude "bioplasma," a theoretical energy field that, under certain conditions, emits charged coherent radiation beyond the body surface in the form of electrons and possibly protons. And although the Soviets did not reach a consensus on the existence of bioplasma, RAND investigators concluded that, "The very pursuit of this theory indicates that Soviet parapsychologists were attempting to explain alleged paranormal phenomena with a greater degree of specificity than their Western counterparts." That extraterrestrials may have developed these extrasensory, bioenergetic powers to a higher degree than could be found among the peoples of Earth was a foregone conclusion. Insofar as the contactees like George Adamski, Howard Menger, Ted Owens and others were concerned, if it was true that they communicated in some fashion with an extraterrestrial or ultra-dimensional intelligence, the monitoring of their activities would fall under the prevue of sundry intelligence agencies.

In returning to the 30 November 1954 memorandum, however, it is extremely important because it deals with the investigation of possible espionage activities. At the behest of the FBI Director, the members of the Detroit club were under intense surveillance because of the claims of some that they were in actual contact with extraterrestrials from a "utopian"- read that communist- civilization on nearby Venus. The FBI needed to make some rapid determinations. First, were there really extraterrestrials living and working among us in the greater Detroit area? Second, were these extraterrestrials in touch with American citizens? Third, if this was the case, what were the intentions of these extraterrestrials? And fourth and lastly, were the humans in any way being empowered and manipulated by the extraterrestrials for the accomplishment of nefarious goals?

The 30 November 1954 memorandum concludes: "In his September 17, 1954 letter, LAUGHEAD states an important date is December 21, 1954, with the center of activity being the Midwest. There will be an earthquake, buildings will fall,

Lake Michigan will rise in a wave extending to Lake Erie, and here and elsewhere, he describes how the entire world will change geologically." Reading this, the FBI needed to immediately ascertain if the earthquake and other disasters were natural or artificially constructed. The memorandum continues to its conclusion: "On November 23, 1954 (DELETED). He inquired whether the FBI was investigating the club, and was advised we could make no statement one way or another regarding the organization. It is not known the date his story will appear.

"The Detroit Office has conducted no investigation of the DFSC, and has received its information from those indicated above, who are voluntarily furnishing it. No investigation of the club is contemplated at this time.

"Detroit has no identifiable subversive information on the officers of the club or of LAUGHEAD or BEIGLOW (also BIGELOW)."

Summary of Adamski Correspondence 26 June 1956, (DELETED) of Seattle, Washington, to FBI Director Hoover: The concerned citizen quotes a paragraph from Waveney Girvan's *Flying Saucers and Common Sense*,[45] regarding a radio interview given by Adamski in which he described some of the FBI's actions to silence him and threats to arrest him if he failed to comply. Jones writes that, "This story sounds unbelievable," and adds that, "I am usually suspicious of anything that appears in a flying saucer book; nevertheless, I want the facts."

The Seattle letter writer particularly wants to know about an alleged visit by three FBI agents who warned Adamski to be quiet about the FBI and the government, and threatened him if he did not; if a warrant for Adamski's arrest had been made and would be served the next time he spoke of such matters on the radio; and lastly, if the story in Girven's book was false, what did the FBI plan to do about it?

10 July 1956, Office Memorandum, Mr. Nichols to A. Jones, Subject: G. Adamski: For a future response to letter from Seattle resident, visits to Adamski by FBI agents are revisited, along with information in the Bureau files with respect to Adamski and his wife, to include warnings from the Bureau about making uncleared public statements concerning it. Adamski's difficulties with the Better Business Bureau (BBB) of Los Angeles, California, were also reviewed, including the FBI's letter to the directors of the business organization pointing out several

---

[45] Waveney Girvan, *Flying Saucers and Common Sense* (New York, New York: Citadel Press, 1956), 120-121.

instances where Adamski was visited by special agents for the purpose of pointing out to him "on no uncertain terms the falsity of his representations." It was indicated that the Air Force was also planning to write a letter to the BBB in Los Angeles to "label Adamski and his works for the fraud they are known to be." It was the recommendation that inquiries concerning George Adamski be forwarded to the BBB Los Angeles chapter.

13 July 1956, Helen W. Gandy, Secretary for Director Hoover, to (DELETED) of Seattle, Washington, regarding George Adamski, suggests that the concerned citizen communicate with the BBB at 1010 Lincoln Bldg., 742 S. Hill St. in Los Angeles, California. On the FBI's copy of this letter are two attached comments from RGE. The first is to the San Diego office referencing their file 100-8382 regarding contacts with Adamski by representatives of their office and OSI and requesting copy of the same. The second is to Mr. Belmont, noting that, "There is no record in Bufiles (Bureau's files) identifiable with correspondent. See Jones to Nichols Memo dated July 10, captioned "George A. Adamski, Palomar Gardens, Valley Center, California." RGE:jfm.

The second comment reveals more about the undemocratic methodology employed by the FBI than anything else. Those citizens who inquire of them are just as scrutinized as suspected criminals. One might suppose that Mr. Hoover and his agents never heard about the Fourth Amendment in the Bill of Rights of the Constitution that provides for "The right of the people to be secure in their persons, houses, papers, and effects, against unreasonable searches and seizures, shall not be violated...." Did this happen to other citizens making inquiries about flying saucers? Was this standard operating procedure or just a special case because it involved questions about George Adamski?

2 August 1956, Letter from (DELETED) of Seattle, Washington, to Director, FBI: In the second letter, the correspondent reports in detail on the BBB of Los Angeles' reply to his letter, which he wrote as Mr. Hoover's secretary, Helen W. Grady, suggested. Essentially, the BBB declared to have no information on Adamski, what he said on radio programs and when or anything else about his books or the claims made in them, and that if the correspondent needed to know more about the activities of FBI agents, he should address his inquiries to the FBI. The correspondent insists that he has not come down in favor of or against the interplanetary hypothesis for flying saucers, but is keeping an open mind. He still desires to write an article for a national magazine soon about George Adamski.

14 August 1956, Office Memorandum to Mr. Nichols from M. A. Jones, Subject: George A. Adamski, Palomar Gardens, Valley Center, California: Jones informs Nichols that the FBI has once again received a letter from the Seattle correspondent in which reference is made a "previous letter he wrote to the Bureau on 6-26-56" asking questions concerning Mr. Adamski's book on flying saucers. He states that the FBI sent the correspondent a letter referring him to the Los Angeles BBB. However, in the second letter, the correspondent is still bothered by "Adamski's claim that he was visited by three FBI Agents and warned to desist in making statements relative to flying saucers or face arrest." Jones comments that the Bureau file 100-395273 does reflect that agents contacted Adamski on two occasions and informed him that he "must desist from inferring that he has any type of approval from the FBI relative to his flying saucer statements." But in the new letter, says Jones, the correspondent "wants to publish an impartial report on flying saucers but states that it is imperative that the FBI answer the question about Adamski being threatened by FBI Agents.

The tone of (DELETED)'s letter is argumentative, and he warns that he will quote in his report any information given to him by the FBI." To this, Jones adds that since the correspondent appeared to be "rather persistent about this matter," that agents should be dispatched to his address to explain that although Adamski was contacted by the FBI, it was only to "suggest he desist in inferring that the FBI cleared his material on space travel." Therefore, the memorandum's recommendation was that the correspondent's letter not be acknowledged, but that agents from the Seattle office be instructed to personally contact him. At attached comment from CSM declares that both the FBI and OSI have supplied the BBB denying any sponsorship of Adamski and denouncing his claims as false.

15 August 1956, letter from Director, FBI, to SAC, Seattle, Subject: George A. Adamski: Attached were the two letters from the Seattle correspondent. Letter goes on to state that, "With respect to his inquiries, you are instructed to have two experienced, mature Agents contact (DELETED) and tactfully inform him that although the FBI did contact Adamski, it was merely to suggest he desist in inferring that the FBI cleared his material on space travel. Inform (DELETED) that the Bureau has no authority to clear any organization, publication or individual and that we certainly have no authority to comment on space travel. He should be informed this was the sole reason for our contact of Adamski…." The Director concluded by expressing his desire that this matter be handled immediately, and that the results of the investigation be transmitted via Airtel immediately.

Airtel Message dated 24 August 1956 from SAC, Seattle (94-267) to Director, FBI, Subject: George A. Adamski, Palomar Gardens, Valley Center, California, Research (Crime Records): Seattle FBI Office refers to "Rebulet, 8/15/56," followed by the deletion of an extensive paragraph. The remainder of Airtel states that on 23 August 1956, special agents did contact the correspondent in the presence of his parents and followed through with the recommendations previously made by M. A. Jones. While the correspondent was disappointed that he was unable to get the answer to his questions in writing, he at least said that he understood the Bureau's position on the matter. The correspondent's parents also indicated considerable concern over the son's involvement in this matter, but admitted that he was "very self-willed and determined to pursue his research on flying saucers," despite their disapproval.

27 November 1959, (DELETED) of Seattle, Washington, to Director, FBI: In the correspondent's third letter he announces a continuance of plans to publish a book about Adamski soon, to be titled *Air Force Evidence Confirms Adamski Story*.[46]

---

[46] September-October 1958 *Flying Saucer Review*, Rickmansworth, United Kingdom, notes that Richard Ogden of Seattle, Washington, was scheduled to self-publish his book in late 1958. The book was never published, however; although another title, *Second Coming of Christ and Flying Saucers*, was self-published by Ogden in 1963 under the banner of Ufology Publications, which Ogden incorporated in Seattle, Washington. The second book sounds a note of alarm regarding the coming Armageddon, warning readers that they should prepare as soon as possible for survival in the last days. Apparently, Ogden's opinions about flying saucers evolved to the point of integrating them into a global Christian perspective. According to the author, the flying saucer occupants need not be physical entities from another planet. They could be the product of supernatural powers, and hence supernatural beings. See Saliba, John A., in James R. Lewis, ed., *Gods Have Landed: New Religions from Other Worlds* (Albany: State University of New York Press, 1995), 25.

Despite the bureaucratic road blocks that the author, whom we now may presume to have been the young man Richard Ogden, encountered from the FBI and other agencies of the federal government, it is apparent that he was still struggling to remain as objective as possible. Ogden wrote, "In this book, *Air Force Evidence Confirms Adamski Story*, it is my intention to present the views of all sides of this controversy. For instance, I have attacked the exposés of Adamski by James W. Moseley, editor of *Saucer News,* and Mr. Lonzo Dove. However, it is not my policy to attack others without allowing them space to reply. Only when the public is allowed to read both sides is it possible to find the truth. I feel that neither side will tell the whole truth but between the conflicting viewpoints lies the truth. This is why I present both sides and leave it up to the reader to separate fiction from fact."

In late 1959, pressure on Adamski was mounting. He was fortunate that a few began to challenge the assertions being made against him in the highest echelons of the federal government; and that among these asking the right questions was Richard Ogden, speaking truth to power. In the letter, the young man enclosed a list of allegations made against the FBI and offered Hoover an opportunity to reply. There were just three allegations that Ogden requested explanations for the purpose of clearing them up and setting the record straight:

1. *That in answer to my letter to you of June 26, 1956 your secretary, Helen W. Gandy, game me false and misleading information and tried to dodge my inquiry.*

2. *That in answer to my letter of August 2, 1956 to you that you sent two agents to my home to lie about Adamski and falsely discredit an innocent man by claiming that he made statements that he never made as proven by a transcription of the tape recording of the radio interview in question, and that he was falsely accused of a crime by your agents who are guilty of hoaxing me.*

3. *That the FBI took part in a conspiracy to intimidate and silence George Adamski on December 17, 1955.*

Ogden points out that Adamski on many occasions praised the FBI and the great work it was doing in protecting America's citizens from the many threats facing them from abroad and at home. So, it surprised him that the FBI would take such an extraordinary interest in muffling Adamski's efforts to tell Americans what he knows about the flying saucers, perhaps providing some clues to solving the mystery of their appearance in our skies. Apparently, Ogden made inquiries about Adamski and UFOs of Allen Dulles, then director of the CIA, and received a more cordial and open response. It is unfortunate that no one has been successful in locating a copy of Dulles' reply to Ogden, insofar as his book was never published, at least to my knowledge and that of other ufologists. Ogden would have surely included any response from Dulles in the pages of his first book.

22 May 1961, letter from (DELETED) in Carmel, California, to J. Edgar Hoover: The author of this letter has read an article by J. Edgar Hoover concerning the connection to con games involving spiritualists and alleged communications with beings from other planets.[47] The correspondent asks about connections between George Adamski and George Hunt Williamson. The correspondent also desires to know if Adamski and Williamson's writings have anything to do with séances and spiritualism. The author of the letter declares that he/she has a friend who informed him/her that they have seen movies of Adamski addressing crowded auditoriums in Great Britain and Holland where some of the crowned heads of Europe were in attendance, paying close attention to every word the contactee uttered. The author also wanted to know if rocket scientist, Dr. Wernher von Braun, was indeed a "constant consultant" of Adamski. The letter writer was concerned about the extent that spiritualism influenced the development of America's space program, in addition to the type of relationship shared by Adamski and von Braun. He/she was also concerned about Williamson's alleged claims to be a European prince from a principality known as Sumadija and asks Director Hoover, "What is this phony business all about, and how dangerous is it to our United States?"

2 June 1961, Director J. Edgar Hoover to (DELETED) in Carmel, California: The Director acknowledges receipt of the letter and expresses appreciation for the interest which prompted the writing of it. Additionally, Hoover explains that, "Although I would like to be of service, the FBI is strictly an investigative agency of the Federal Government and neither makes evaluations nor draws conclusions as to the character or integrity of any organization, publication or individual." He goes

---

[47]   J. Edgar Hoover, "From the Files of the FBI…. The Strange Case of the Swindler from Outer Space," 21 May 1961, *Chronicle,* San Francisco, California.

on to explain that he regrets not being able to help the letter writer whose opinion was so favorable to the Director's newspaper article, and states that he hopes that the letter writer would "not infer in this connection either that we do or do not have data in our files relating to the matter about which you asked." Hoover encloses a recent statement that he made concerning both Adamski and Williamson that he felt might be helpful to the writer:

Enclosure

4-17-61 Statement re Internal Security

NOTE: Bufiles contain nothing of a derogatory nature concerning (DELETED) with whom there has been one previous contact on 4-12-49 at which time she was given a no-jurisdiction-type reply. Bufiles indicate that George Hunt Williamson and George Adamski have come to the Bureau's attention in the past in connection with allegations that flying disks exist. In 1954, Williamson was connected with a program to be presented in Cincinnati which was entitled "The Real Flying Saucer Story." Adamski is the author of a book entitled "Flying Saucers Have Landed" which was published by Werner-Lowery Company in England in 1953. HHA:pia(3)

Analysis: Director Hoover is concerned about the existence of flying saucers insofar as these objects may pose a threat to national security. He is also wary of any connections with that the contactees may have with spiritualist scheming, which up to that time largely fell under the prevue of bunko squad investigators in local police departments. While Jack Parsons, one of the founders of the Jet Propulsion Laboratory, was steeped in occult and spiritualistic practices, it should be noted that he passed away on 17 June 1952, as the result of a mysterious explosion while working on some pyrotechnics for a Hollywood movie. Nevertheless, the extent that occult organizations influenced our rocket scientists and space pioneers in 1961 would have been a matter of deep interest for the Director and the FBI, insofar as these were the professionals on the cutting edge of advanced technological developments and then working on the preparation of the first space probe to another planet, the Mariner which was scheduled for a fly-by of Venus. We were in a race with the Soviets to be the first to send a spacecraft to another world. That the communists could use occultism as a segway to get into the minds of our space scientists, Director Hoover would not put it past them.

For many years following the death of Adamski, the documents presented herein not only remain classified, but were checked out, initialed and stamped dozens of times. In the interests of national security, there are probably many more FBI documents pertinent to George Adamski and his experiences in addition to other contactees and their encounters with an extraterrestrial or ultradimensional intelligence, the true X-files. In 1975, just three years after J. Edgar Hoover passed away and ten years after Adamski's death, it was revealed that the FBI was intently involved with the investigation of UFO phenomena all along and at every level. John M. Webb, a reporter for the *National Enquirer*, declared in the 1 July 1975 edition of that newspaper that, "In the staid FBI Law Enforcement Bulletin- which goes to 80,000 agents and police officials- an article instructed police to relay citizen reports of UFO sightings over a secret toll-free number to the privately operated Center for UFO Studies in Northridge, Illinois."

When an FBI spokesperson, Ed Gooderham, was asked why they ran that UFO article in the bulletin, noted that it was crucial to do this because most people turn to the local police when they see something out of the ordinary. "We recognize it's a police responsibility to look into UFO reports," he asserted. The spokesperson also justified the article on the grounds that the FBI was trying to help scientists find out the answer to the UFO phenomenon.

Dr. J. Allen Hynek, the author of the article, as well as an astronomer from Northwestern University in Illinois and former consultant to the United States Air Force *Project Bluebook*, was then serving as the Director of the Center for UFO Studies. "I have no doubt," said the esteemed scientist, "that this further cooperation from law-enforcement agencies could bring us closer to a solution of the great UFO mystery."

His article provided detailed instructions as to how the police should utilize the 24-hour UFO hotline to call in accurate descriptions of UFOs and any possible physical effects the objects may exert on people, plants, animals, cars and communications. The astronomer noted that when a determination was made at the center that a particular UFO sighting or encounter was important enough, eyewitnesses would be interviewed as quickly as possible by trained UFO investigators; and that these would also conduct an extensive survey and examination of the area where the UFO was sighted or encountered.

Hynek's detailed guidelines also appeared in the American Federation of Police publications, *Police Times* and the *Police and Fire Journal.* These are read by over 23,000 fire chiefs, 17,000 police chiefs 3,000 sheriffs. Hynek commented that, "Of the calls we've received over the hot line from police, 25 percent involve UFO sightings made by the police themselves. Five years ago, very few officers would have reported seeing a UFO because they would have been laughed at. Now, no matter how bizarre a person's story, the police tend to check it out- and often see for themselves." Hynek concluded, "With police participation, we're getting better data because officers are trained observers."

Gerald Arenberg, the executive director of the American Federation of Police, announced that, "The fact that the FBI took the opportunity to endorse the project proves there is credibility in UFO investigation. It's natural for people to turn to police for assistance after a UFO sighting; and law-enforcement agencies must be ready to handle reports effectively." He also said that it was now the official policy of the Federation of Police for members to provide information on UFOs to scientists and to use the UFO center's hot line. Therefore, if the FBI and local police and fire departments were content with chasing lights in the sky, they were at least serving to create the illusion that the government was doing something about getting down to the truth about flying saucers. Hynek's deeper involvement with both the UFO phenomenon and the Venus conspiracy is explained at greater lengths in *Venus Rising.*[48]

FBI's Continued UFO Involvement

UFOs, now more commonly referred to by various government agencies as "unidentified aerial phenomena" (UAPs), have captured the public's attention for nearly eight decades. While the Air Force brass initially dismissed UFO reports as "hoaxes, misinterpretations of natural phenomena or the misidentification of conventional aircraft as seen through unusual atmospheric conditions," declassified FBI documents such as those pertaining to the case of George Adamski, reveal the government took sightings seriously and devoted vast resources to investigating them.

---

[48]   Keller, *Venus Rising*, 175. Revelations given to Brazilian space researcher Débora Bergara in Argentina by Hynek upon his visit to Entre Rios province are detailed.

The FBI's involvement began in 1947 following a rash of widely publicized UFO sightings across America. FBI Director J. Edgar Hoover felt that his agents should cooperate with the Air Force in verifying sightings if so requested by the top brass in that newly-minted military branch. By July 1950, the Air Force no longer wanted the FBI's assistance, however, declaring that, "The jurisdiction and responsibility for investigating flying saucers have been assumed by the United States Air Force."

Despite the top echelon of the Air Force wanting to assume total responsibility for UFO investigations, declassified memos show the FBI displaying a significant interest in the subject. In one 1950 memo, Guy Hottel, head of the FBI's Washington, D.C. field office, relayed an unconfirmed report about three disc-shaped craft that crashed with crew members resembling humans recovered at three locations in New Mexico: Roswell, the Plains of San Augustin, and Aztec. While the FBI, so far as we have been able to determine, never investigated these incidents, the memo reveals that agents of the FBI were at least gathering intelligence on UFOs. Another memo received by the FBI in 1947, dispatched from an Army general to Hoover, confirms military officials were also taking reports seriously by contacting the FBI for its agents to investigate sightings. Declassified CIA documents from the 1940s-1990s reveal that both CIA agents (foreign-based) and FBI agents (domestic) were instructed to gather UFO reports, though most described unsubstantiated sightings from press reports rather than direct evidence.

While the Air Force was the lead investigative body on UFO sightings, the FBI continued to play a role, particularly when UFOs entered restricted airspace. According to declassified records, from 1947-1969, the Air Force conducted UFO investigations under Project Blue Book. Their files include over 12,000 sightings, with over 700 remaining unidentified. The project's termination in 1969 was not due to a belief sightings had stopped, but rather a judgement that the existing reports revealed "no threat or scientific value." Supposedly, the FBI was no longer formally investigating UFOs. However, declassified documents prove the FBI continued monitoring sightings, especially reports of objects near sensitive military installations. FBI records reveal that its agents were interviewing UFO witnesses and experiencers, and gathering material on sightings from the largest civilian UFO group, the National Investigations Committee on Aerial Phenomena (NICAP). A 1973 memo from the FBI Director recommended a scientist contact NICAP about UFO photographic analysis, rather than the FBI directly. The FBI felt secure in utilizing the scientific consultancy of NICAP, realizing that many on the NICAP board of directors shared backgrounds in the United States intelligence community, active and retired. Apparently, the FBI acted as an interested party in monitoring UFO activity across America, especially in cases where sightings occurred near critical infrastructure sites or sensitive airspace.

Recent Developments

The United States government has shown renewed interest in UFOs/UAPs following sightings reported by military pilots and the revelation of a secret Pentagon program investigating the phenomenon. The public outcry for UFO disclosure led to Congress requiring the Director of National Intelligence to produce an unclassified report on UAPs. The 25 June 2021 preliminary assessment examined 144 sightings and concluded that most cases represented "physical objects exhibiting unusual flight characteristics with no clear earthly explanation."[49]

80 years of FBI documents attest to the Bureau's agents actively monitoring and investigating UFO sightings, most notably when reports may have represented threats or unknown technologies. Of course, the government now admits some UAPs display advanced capabilities, thereby raising questions about their origins and intentions. If sightings continue unabated and detection improves, these phenomena will surely reveal secrets about advanced foreign adversaries or something more profound. Even though the truth so far remains elusive, the FBI documentation makes it clear the United States government has never fully ignored the UAP issue and will continue analyzing credible sightings and close encounters of every kind.

---

[49] Author unstated, "Declassified: What the FBI Knows About UFOs," *New Space Economy,* 5 February 2024, Department of Justice Website | *New Space Economy,* (Accessed 21 July 2025).

APPENDIX B

POST-UFO ENCOUNTER TRAVAILS OF PORTAGE COUNTY, OHIO DEPUTY SHERIFF DALE SPAUR

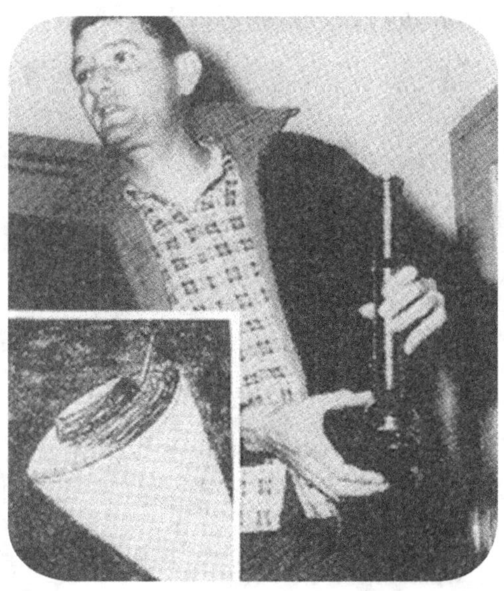

Portage County, Ohio, Deputy Sheriff Dale F. Spaur describes the shape and size of flying saucer as seen at arm's length during his police car chase of a UFO from Ravenna, Ohio, to the outskirts of Pittsburgh, Pennsylvania, a total of 86 miles, during the early morning of 17 April 1966. Photo and drawing at inset done by Spaur as it appeared in the *Cleveland Scene* magazine.

In the days, weeks, months and even years following the 17 April 1966 UFO encounter of Portage County, Ohio, Deputy Sheriff Dale Spaur and Special Deputy W. L. (Barney) Neff, Deputy Sheriff Spaur was plagued with the consequences of reporting the details of the encounter. Special Deputy Neff, on the other hand, escaped the resulting long-term media onslaught simply by refusing the discuss the UFO incident. Anytime he was asked about it, all Neff would say is, "No comment."

For Spaur, the end of the saucer chase was the beginning of a life-long nightmare. No sooner than his return to the Portage County Sheriff's Office in Ravenna, Ohio, he and his partner Neff were besieged by newspaper reporters, radio and television broadcasters, government officials from sundry levels of the state and national bureaucracy, in addition to investigators from the United States Air Force, all desiring to hear their complete story. Since Spaur was the only one of the police pair to oblige them, he became the focus of all media attention. Constantly being bombarded by questions about the UFO chase from media representatives and other interested parties, day-after-day, Spaur could no longer effectively serve Portage County in his capacity as the Deputy Sheriff. The frenzy was such that an anonymous article in *UFOs 67* magazine, Issue No. 1, "The Ordeal of Dale Spaur: The Flying Sauer that Wrecked a Home," Tom McArdell, editor (New York, New York: K.M.R. Publications, 1 January 1967), noted that, "Letters poured into headquarters from all parts of the world, advising them (Officers Spaur and Neff) what to do if 'little green men' should try to contact them. Star-gazers and saucer worshippers called him (Spaur) on the phone day and night, giving him no time that he could really call his own. And soon his job was being filled by someone else."

Spaur sadly summed up this onslaught: "My entire life came crashing down around my shoulders. Everything changed. I still don't know what happened. But suddenly, it was as though I no longer had anything for myself. My wife, my home, my two children- They all seemed to fade away." It was all just too much for Spaur's wife, Daneise, who filed for divorce.

Apparently, Daneise was reluctant to file for divorce, but felt she had run out of options. She told a local newspaper reporter, "Something happened to Dale, but I don't know what it was. He came home that day, and I never saw him more frightened before. He acted strange, listless. He just sat around. He was very pale. Then later, he got nervous, and he started to run away. He'd just disappear for days and days. I wouldn't see him. Our marriage fell apart. All sorts of people came to the house. Investigators, reporters. They kept him up all night. They kept after him, hounding him. They hounded him right into the ground. And he changed."

That four other police officers in Northeast Ohio sighted the flying saucer on that eventful April morning made little difference. They, too, were hounded by media representatives, although not quite as intently as Spaur. There was also political pressure from local elected officials who did not like their police officers speeding along the highways in pursuit of flying saucers.

With Spaur's marriage finished and finding himself standing in the unemployment line, to get back on his feet he found work in nearby Solon, Ohio, as a painter, to which he had to walk three miles to the job site every day from a hotel room that cost him $60 per week. He earned but a meager $80 per week, and the court ordered him to pay the remaining $20 for child support. He lost 40 pounds in this ordeal. When all was said and done, the legacy of his UFO close encounter left Spaur ridiculed and flat broke.

No wonder why so many law enforcement officials are still hesitant to discuss their own UFO encounters.

Dale Floyd Spaur (1932-1984) was very tall, at 6'7". He always stood out in a crowd. In the Portage County Sheriff's Department, he was noted for a "wicked sense of humor." An Air Force veteran, Spaur was a gunner on a B-51 in the Korean War. After many years of moving back and forth between his native West Virginia and Ohio, taking up odd jobs, Spaur remarried a Cleveland woman and finally managed to secure his own business, a bar in the Cleveland, Ohio, suburb of Rocky River, where he could finally put the saga of the great flying saucer chase behind him "in a cloud of dust on Ohio State Route 224," as country music star Jo Dee Messina might sing.